'It's windier up here than down in the city. You're obviously getting cold,' Ryan said.

'Oh, a few minutes won't hurt. I want to see the site for your future home,' Carolyn said, then shivered.

Ryan encircled her with his arms, stepping close to nestle her to him. Carolyn stiffened for a moment, then relaxed, savouring the warmth of Ryan's massive, powerful body.

Oh, he was so strong, yet so gentle. She was definitely not cold any longer. The heat emanating from Ryan was suffusing her, causing her heart to quicken its tempo. The heat was growing hotter, beginning to burn within her with licking flames of desire.

Move away, Carolyn, she ordered herself. This was dangerous, was too intimate and… It was as though she and Ryan had been transported to another world where no one existed but the two of them. And in this world, they were free to do whatever felt right and real.

Available in November 2003 from Silhouette Special Edition

Good Husband Material
by Susan Mallery
(Hometown Heartbreakers)

Tall, Dark and Irresistible
by Joan Elliott Pickart
(The Baby Bet: MacAllister's Gifts)

My Secret Wife
by Cathy Gillen Thacker
(The Deveraux Legacy)

An American Princess
by Tracy Sinclair

Lt Kent: Lone Wolf
by Judith Lyons

The Stranger She Married
by Crystal Green
(Kane's Crossing)

Tall, Dark and Irresistible

JOAN ELLIOTT PICKART

SILHOUETTE®
SPECIAL EDITION™

For Autumn and Kate,
special little ladies
of two worlds.

*Silhouette, Silhouette Special Edition and Colophon are
registered trademarks of Harlequin Books S.A., used under licence.*

*First published in Great Britain 2003
Silhouette Books, Eton House, 18-24 Paradise Road,
Richmond, Surrey TW9 1SR*

© Joan Elliott Pickart 2002

ISBN 0 373 24507 6

23-1103

*Printed and bound in Spain
by Litografía Rosés S.A., Barcelona*

JOAN ELLIOTT PICKART

is the author of over eighty-five novels. When she isn't writing, she enjoys reading, gardening and attending craft shows with her young daughter, Autumn. Joan also has three all-grown-up daughters and three fantastic grandchildren. Joan and Autumn live in a charming small town in the high pine country of Arizona.

THE MACALLISTER FAMILY TREE

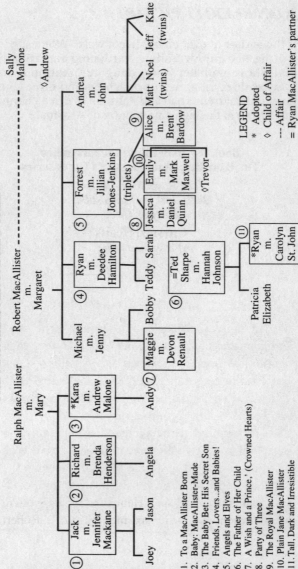

LEGEND

* Adopted
◇ Child of Affair
--- Affair
= Ryan MacAllister's partner

1. To a MacAllister Born
2. Baby: MacAllister-Made
3. The Baby Bet: His Secret Son
4. Friends, Lovers...and Babies!
5. Angels and Elves
6. The Father of Her Child
7. A Wish and a Prince,' (Crowned Hearts)
8. Party of Three
9. The Royal MacAllister
10. Plain Jane MacAllister
11. Tall, Dark and Irresistible

Prologue

"I'm here as summoned," Ryan Sharpe said, smiling as he sank onto the butter-soft leather chair next to the fireplace in Robert MacAllister's study. His grandfather sat in a matching chair across from Ryan, the leaping flames of a warming fire crackling in the hearth separating the two men.

"I'm honored to be included as one of your grandchildren in your secret mission to give each of us a special gift at a time of your choosing."

"You know that I've considered you my grandson ever since Ted and Hannah adopted you in Korea when you were six months old," Robert said. "The Sharpe family had always been a part of the ever-growing MacAllister clan.

"I'm very proud of you, Ryan. You've worked extremely hard and are a valued member of the team at MacAllister Architects." He chuckled. "And like the others who have already received their gifts, you're early for our meeting."

Ryan laughed.

"As you know, it's up to you whether you choose to tell anyone what I give you this evening. That's entirely your decision to make."

Ryan nodded.

Robert frowned and studied Ryan for a long moment before speaking again, causing Ryan to shift uncomfortably in his chair under his grandfather's intense scrutiny.

"I wish I had some magical words to say to you, or a mystical wand to wave," Robert finally said quietly, "that would create peace within you, Ryan. I've watched you struggle with your mixed heritage for so many years, and it's heartbreaking to know you feel as though you don't really fit in here—or in Korea."

Ryan sighed. "I hoped that the trip I just made to Korea would bring me that peace, make me feel as though I'd found the place where I really belong, but it just didn't happen.

"So, here I am, half and half, not fitting in anywhere. People stared at me in Korea because I'm six feet tall like my birth father and have wavy brown hair, yet my eyes are almond shaped like my birth mother, and my skin is tawny. The journey to Korea only emphasized to me that I'm different.''

"Mmm," Robert said, nodding.

"Please don't misunderstand me, Grandpa," Ryan said, leaning forward. "I have the greatest, most loving parents that any guy could have. I'm very grateful for them and for the entire Mac-Allister family. My problems are my own. I'm beginning to believe, though, that I'm never going to get a handle on this war I continually fight within myself."

"Which brings us to the subject of your special gift," Robert said, getting to his feet.

He crossed the room to his desk and returned to settle again in the chair, holding a white box that was approximately a ten-inch cube. He stared at the box, then extended it toward Ryan.

"I give you this with love," Robert said, "and pray that it helps you quiet your demons."

Ryan set the box on his thighs, then carefully removed the lid. He pushed back the white tissue paper, then his breath caught. With hands that were not quite steady he reached in and gently withdrew the special gift.

It was a globe.

Nestled on a dark, wooden stand was an exquisite, intricately detailed antique globe, the creation being a total of about seven inches tall. It was made of such fine china that the glow of the flames from the fire could be seen through the sphere.

"It's...it's beautiful," Ryan said, awe ringing in his voice. "Absolutely incredible. I...I don't know what to say, Grandpa."

"Then just listen to me please, Ryan," Robert said quietly, as he leaned forward. "You're holding the world in your hands at this very moment. Don't you see that you are so much bigger than it is, than the prejudices that world might have?

"The whole world is yours. Oh, my dear boy, don't be so driven to find your place in it, to feel that you must choose between your two unique cultures. Embrace them both, realize how blessed you are to have them. Each gives you rare and wonderful gifts. Accept who you are and be at peace.

"I hope that whenever you look at the globe, you'll remember what I've said tonight. I pray that it will ease your pain and make your path easier in the future. I love you, Ryan."

"I love..." Ryan said, then tears filled his eyes. "I love you, too, Grandpa. I'll treasure this gift for the rest of my life, and I swear to you that I'll try even harder to find that inner peace. I'll look at this globe every day and hear your words and... thank you.''

Ryan swallowed heavily. ''But thank you isn't big enough to express how I feel. You put so much thought and love into choosing this globe for me and...'' Emotions closed his throat and he shook his head.

''Your thank-you will do just fine,'' Robert said, smiling. ''Now, go home, Ryan. Take your globe...your world...with you, along with a firm resolve to become a man at peace with who and what he is. God bless you, my beloved grandson. Good night.''

Ryan nodded, replaced the globe carefully in the box, covered it and got to his feet. Unable to speak past the lump in his throat he gazed at his grandfather and saw tears matching his own shimmering in the older man's eyes.

After a long moment, Ryan turned and walked from the room, closing the door behind him with a quiet click.

Chapter One

One Year Later

Hands across the Sea International Adoptions was located on the fourth floor of an office building in Ventura, but was bursting at the seams and needed more office space. A new spacious structure was going to be on a piece of land donated by a grateful couple who were overjoyed with their newly adopted daughter. Ryan had agreed to present the plans for another architect at the firm who was still on vacation.

He entered the office and glanced around, de-

ciding immediately that he liked the classy but
welcoming reception area that had been decorated
in colors of country blue and raspberry. Numerous
plants gave it a homey touch, and a play area in a
corner was equipped with toys, a small table and
chairs. He approached the smiling receptionist and
gave her his name and the purpose of his visit.

"Oh, yes, Mr. Sharpe," the young woman said,
"they're expecting you, but we're running a little
late this morning. If you don't mind waiting in Ms.
St. John's office, she'll be with you in just a few
minutes. Carolyn St. John is our assistant director,
and is in charge of Asian adoptions. The head of
the agency is tied up in an overseas conference
call."

"No problem," Ryan said. "Just point me in
the right direction."

The receptionist got to her feet. "I'll show you
the way. Would you care for a cup of coffee or
tea?"

Ryan declined the offer and was deposited in a
large office decorated in the same colors as the
front area. A stack of files was on top of a desk,
filing cabinets lined one wall and two chairs were
placed in front of the desk. He leaned the cardboard tube against one of the chairs, then his
glance fell on the wall behind the desk.

There were more than two dozen framed photographs of Asian children ranging in age from, Ryan guessed, maybe two or three months up to eight or nine years displayed on the wall. He frowned as he slowly studied each photograph, his gaze lingering on the pictures of the older children.

Memories from years ago hammered against his mind, causing him to feel a chill.

He was seven or eight years old and seated in a restaurant booth with his adoptive parents and older sister, Patty, who was a carbon copy of their mother.

He saw the speculative looks from the other diners as they scrutinized the Sharpes, then whispered among themselves. He was sure they were saying that, for some unknown reason, his parents had decided to complete their family by adding a foreign child, who stuck out like a sore thumb.

He recalled an open-house night in elementary school during which his teacher commented that she hadn't realized Ryan was a foster child, then apologized quickly when Ted informed her that Ryan was their son.

He remembered the day that Patty had come home from school in tears, saying some of the older kids had taunted her, saying her mother must have been getting it on with the gardener or the grocery man. They couldn't imagine why Patty would have such a weird-looking younger brother who obviously wasn't really a Sharpe.

Then later in high school... No, enough of this. Enough.

Ryan shook his head to fling into oblivion the disturbing images of days long past, drew a deep, steadying breath, then stared at the photographs again.

Carolyn St. John rushed to the open doorway of her office, prepared to apologize to Mr. Sharpe for keeping him waiting. She stopped so abruptly she teetered slightly and completely forgot what she was going to say.

My goodness, she thought, as she swept her gaze over the man standing in front of her desk. Mr. Ryan Sharpe was, without a doubt, one of the most handsome, well-built men she had ever seen.

He was, she guessed, about six feet tall, had dark brown, wavy hair, tawny skin, and drop-dead gorgeous, extremely dark, almond-shaped eyes. His suit was obviously custom-tailored and accentuated his broad shoulders and long, muscular legs.

There was an—oh, what should she call it—a blatant masculinity emanating from Ryan Sharpe, a sensual male something that was causing her heart to do a funny little flutter and a flush of heat to stain her cheeks.

Well, this was ridiculous, to say the least, Carolyn thought, drawing a much-needed breath. She was reacting to Mr. Sharpe like an adolescent girl who found herself in a dither because she was in close proximity to the popular football quarterback in high school. Enough of this nonsense.

"I'm sorry to have—" Carolyn started, as she walked forward. She stopped speaking as she heard the breathy quality of her voice, cleared her throat and tried again. "—kept you waiting, Mr. Sharpe.

"I'm Carolyn St. John. The others are waiting for us in the conference room to review the plans you're presenting for the new building. Our director, Elizabeth Kane, will join us as soon as she finishes with an overseas telephone call. Were you offered something to drink?"

Ryan pulled his gaze from the photographs and turned to look at Carolyn St. John.

Pretty woman, he thought immediately. Really lovely. Carolyn St. John was about five foot six, slender, had curly dark hair that sort of fluffed around her face and fell to just below her ears and the bluest eyes he had ever seen. Nice. Very, very nice.

She was wearing a long-sleeved blue dress that matched her eyes with a swirly-looking skirt that came to just below her knees and revealed shapely calves and ankles. Her only jewelry was a gold locket on a delicate chain.

But he'd been so engrossed in looking at the pictures on the wall that he hadn't heard one word she had said beyond asking if he'd been offered refreshments.

"Yes, thank you, but I don't care for anything to drink," he said, smiling slightly. He switched his gaze back to the wall of pictures. "I assume these are children from overseas that have been adopted by their new American parents."

"Yes, they are," Carolyn said, closing the distance between them.

Oh, Ryan Sharpe smelled good, too, she thought rather giddily. He was wearing a woodsy-scented aftershave that suited him perfectly.

"I'm in charge of Asian adoptions," she said, "as well as being the assistant director of the agency. Those are photographs of children from various Asian countries I've placed with couples and single people in the States." She smiled. "It's my gallery of happiness and dreams come true."

"Happiness and dreams come true," Ryan said quietly, but with a slight edge to his voice, "for the parents. I qualify to have my baby picture on a wall like that because my parents adopted me from Korea."

Ryan paused and looked at Carolyn St. John again, a deep frown on his face.

"I know you believe you're performing a service here by providing these children with a chance at a life far better than the one they would have had in an orphanage," he went on, "and you are, to a point.

"But have you ever considered the far-reaching ramifications, Ms. St. John, of placing foreign children with American parents? Have you thought about what it's like for those kids when they realize they are different, just don't fit in? Do you ever think about that, when you're handing out cute little babies from overseas?"

"First of all, Mr. Sharpe," Carolyn said, with a flash of anger, "we don't *hand out* those children to just anyone. You're obviously only part Korean but..." She planted her hands on her hips. "I'm sorry if you had difficulties with your mixed-heritage while growing up, but no, I'm not going to justify what I do here, to someone who has a chip on his shoulder as wide as Toledo."

Carolyn narrowed her eyes and lifted her chin. "If you'll follow me, please," she said coolly, "we'll join the others and you can present the plans for the new building."

Carolyn spun around and marched from the room.

"Hey, I'm sorry. I…" Ryan stopped speaking as Carolyn disappeared from view. "Damn."

Ryan shook his head in self-disgust, then grabbed the cardboard cylinder. He stared up at the ceiling for a long moment, then drew a deep breath, letting it out slowly with the hope of dispelling the anger he felt for his behavior.

Man, he thought, who had put a rotten nickel in him, causing him to mouth off like that? Those photographs had caused painful memories to rise up from some dusty corner of his mind and slam against him like physical blows.

But that was no excuse for what he had just done and said. Not only had he represented MacAllister Architects very poorly, he had also alienated a very attractive woman. A woman, who when angry, had eyes like incredible blue laser beams and a pretty flush on her cheeks.

He had to apologize to Carolyn St. John, make amends…right now.

Ryan left the office and looked down a hallway, seeing Carolyn waiting for him at the far end of the corridor. She had her arms crossed beneath her breasts and was tapping the toe of one shoe impatiently.

She was definitely angry at him, Ryan thought, starting toward her, not smiling.

Ryan strode down the hall and stopped in front of Carolyn.

"Look, I want to say that I..." he started.

"The others are seated inside," Carolyn said, cutting him off as she spoke to the knot of his tie. "We're running late as it is, so shall we go in, Mr. Sharpe?"

"It's Ryan and..."

Carolyn swept one arm through the air. "After you. I'm just breathless with anticipation to hear what other pearly words of wisdom you have to offer...Mr. Sharpe."

Ryan cringed as Carolyn's words made a direct hit on his already guilty conscious, and he moved past her to enter the large room where a dozen people were seated around a long table.

Carolyn introduced Ryan to Elizabeth who introduced Ryan to the others as Carolyn took a seat at the far end. As Ryan spread out the blueprints in the center of the table, everyone got to their feet to see better. Carolyn rose but stayed at the edge of the group.

Ryan Sharpe, she fumed, might be one of the most handsome and well-built men she had ever encountered, but big macho deal. All the rugged good looks and nicely placed muscles in the world would not erase the fact that she *did not* like him.

How dare he pass negative judgment on her and

the agency? He accused her of not knowing what it was like to be different? Oh, ha, a lot he knew. She had firsthand knowledge of that lonely status.

But no matter what difficulties he might have had while growing up, and no matter what problems the precious children she helped place with parents in this country might encounter, they were far better off here than lost in the shuffle in overcrowded orphanages and—

Oh, Carolyn, shut up, she told herself. She didn't have to justify her chosen career to a narrowminded hunk with an attitude. So there.

"Right," Carolyn said decisively, then realized, to her embarrassment as everyone turned to look at her, that she'd spoken aloud.

"Well, good, Carolyn," Elizabeth said, smiling. "I'm glad you agree that French doors leading to the courtyard are much classier than what we'd decided on earlier. It appears we're in accord, Mr. Sharpe."

"It's Ryan, please," he said to Elizabeth, then shifted his attention to Carolyn. "I'm delighted that you and I are on the same page…Carolyn."

"Oh, we are…Ryan," she said, ever so sweetly. "About French doors."

Elizabeth frowned. "Did I miss something here, Carolyn?"

"No, Elizabeth," Carolyn said, "nothing that

deserves any further discussion. Are there any other changes from the original ideas we presented that we need to be apprised of?''

''Well, no, not according to the notes I was given,'' Ryan said. ''I just need Elizabeth to sign off on these plans and we're all set. You can present these blueprints to your contractor. Mac-Allister Architects will have another set on file at our office in case any questions or problems arise during construction.''

''We're going to have a ground-breaking ceremony with the press invited,'' Elizabeth said. ''I think I'll buy a shiny shovel and put a huge red bow on it to turn over the first scoop of soil on our land and…''

As Elizabeth chattered on to Ryan about the ground-breaking ceremony, he smiled and nodded, then watched in frustration as Carolyn left the room without making eye contact with him.

At last able to escape, Ryan hurried to Carolyn's office where she was sitting at her desk busily typing on a computer keyboard. Ryan stood in front of the desk and cleared his throat. Carolyn continued to type.

''Carolyn,'' Ryan said finally.

''Hmm?'' she said, her fingers flying over the keys.

''Look, I'm sorry about what I said earlier. I was

way out of line, and I apologize for my outburst. It's just that I... No, there's no excuse for my behavior. I'd like to make amends. Would you have lunch with me? I'll come back at noon and pick you up. Please?''

Carolyn stopped typing, pressed a key to save the work, then turned her head slowly to meet Ryan's gaze.

"Lunch?" he repeated, producing his best one-hundred-watt smile. "Please, Carolyn?"

"I bet you're accustomed to getting just about anything you want with that smile...Ryan," she said. "Well, chalk this up as a new experience for you. Have lunch? With you? Do let me know if there's any part of this reply to your request that you don't understand, but my answer is really quite simple. No.''

Chapter Two

That night Ryan sat in his favorite chair in his living room, an open and forgotten book on his lap as he stared into space, frowning.

Carolyn St. John, he mused. The events that had transpired earlier continued to haunt him. In the silence of his apartment, there was no way to escape from again squaring off against his less-than-flattering behavior hours before.

Ryan sighed, leaned his head on the top of the chair and glowered at the ceiling.

Yes, he'd come a long way, since receiving the globe from his grandfather, toward achieving his goal of finding an inner peace about his heritage. But what he had done that morning was screaming the fact that he still had miles to go in his quest.

Even more disturbing, he mentally raged on, was the negative impression he'd made on Carolyn. He'd slam-dunked that lovely woman in an area of her life that was obviously of great importance to her. He'd infuriated her and very possibly hurt her, as well.

No wonder she'd refused to go to lunch with him. He was lucky that she hadn't popped him in the chops.

Ryan set the book on the table next to him, got to his feet and began to pace restlessly around the large room, now and then dragging one hand through his hair.

He couldn't just erase from his mind what had happened and go about his business. He had to make amends to Carolyn, not only to ease his conscience but because...well, because he was attracted to Carolyn and hoped the lack of a ring on her finger meant she was single and not involved with anyone.

Carolyn St. John, Ryan thought, continuing his trek, was a very intriguing woman. Her slender, small-boned stature gave the initial impression that this was a woman who needed protecting from harm's way, should be taken care of, because she was...delicate.

But, oh, man, there was far more to Carolyn than the first glimpse would indicate. There was a depth to her, layers that beckoned to be discovered, one by one.

She was passionate, there was no other word for it—about her career, about the families she formed by uniting orphans from overseas with people who had empty arms and were aching to have a child to love and cherish.

She had a temper...oh, brother, did she ever... when an emotional button of importance to her was pushed by an idiot like himself who dared do such a stupid thing.

She was stubborn. He'd done everything he could think of at the time to set things right, mend fences, make amends for his crummy behavior, but she wasn't having any of it, no way. She'd lifted that pert little chin of hers, nailed him in place with those expressive, dynamite blue eyes of hers and refused to go to lunch with him. She had said no in such a way that he'd known he had better hit the road while he still could.

"Oh, yeah, she's really something," Ryan said, slouching back onto his chair. "But, Carolyn, my sweet? I may have lost that battle, but this war isn't over yet. Not by a long shot."

*   *   *

With a weary sigh Carolyn entered her bedroom, eager to slip into bed and end this day that had seemed to be a week long.

That darn Ryan Sharpe, she thought, as she removed her dress, had taken up residency in her brain. Why was she wasting mental energy on a man she didn't even like? He was rude and opinionated. He'd dumped emotional baggage on her about his heritage and practically condemned what she was devoted to, heart and soul and mind.

Clad in her slip, Carolyn crossed the room, plunked her elbows on the top of the dresser and scrutinized her reflection in the mirror with a critical eye.

What, she wondered, had Ryan Sharpe seen as a man looking at a woman for the first time? Well, she'd been told over the years that she was pretty, and she was, she supposed. Not gorgeous, nor stunning, and definitely not voluptuous, just sort of wholesome, picture-on-a-box-of-corn-flakes pretty.

Ryan was the type of man who could have his pick of gorgeous, stunning and voluptuous women. He no doubt drew women like bees to honey.

A chill swept through Carolyn as Ryan's scathing words echoed in her mind.

"Stop it," Carolyn said aloud, realizing she was close to tears. She wrapped her hands around her elbows and drew a steadying breath. "Oh, yes, Ryan Sharpe, I know all about being different, not fitting in. Being different, different, different."

With a wobbly sigh that held the echo of tears, and with hands that trembled slightly, Carolyn reached up and removed her double hearing aids.

Three days later in the middle of the morning, Carolyn rolled her eyes heavenward and frowned as a young woman entered Carolyn's office carrying a bouquet of flowers in a pearly blue vase.

"Oh, no, Janice," Carolyn said, leaning back in her chair and covering her eyes. "Not again."

"Peekaboo, these are for you," Janice said merrily. "Again. This is the third bouquet in as many days, Carolyn. Everyone in the office is just buzzing with curiosity as to who your new suitor is." She set the vase on Carolyn's desk. "Whisper his name to me. I swear I won't tell more than ten people who he is."

Carolyn laughed. "Oh, really? That's an offer I can barely refuse, but I'll force myself to pass."

"Well, darn it," Janice said, then removed the small white envelope from the plastic holder and waved it in the air. "How much is this worth to you without my peeking first?"

"Your life." Carolyn extended one hand and wiggled her fingers. "Give."

"Shoot," Janice said, then dropped the envelope into Carolyn's palm. "The romance of the century is taking place here and we only know the identity of one half of the dewy-eyed couple. You."

"I am *not* half of a dewy-eyed couple, for Pete's sake. Goodbye."

As soon as Janice left, Carolyn dropped the envelope onto the top of her desk and stared at it as she toyed with the idea of just tearing it in two and throwing it in the trash. She knew exactly what would be written on the card, as it would no doubt be the same words as the previous two cards that had arrived with the gorgeous flowers.

Carolyn, she mentally recited, *I'm sorry. Please forgive me and agree to have lunch with me. Ryan.*

"Oh, he's driving me over the edge," Carolyn said, snatching up the envelope and taking out the card. "Yep, there it is. 'Carolyn, I'm sorry. Please forgive me and agree to have lunch with me. Ryan.' Well, I've had enough of this, thank you very much."

She removed the telephone book from the bottom drawer of her desk, plunked it on the desk and began to flip through the pages with more force than was necessary. When she found the number she wanted, she punched them on the telephone and heard the ringing on the other end of the line.

"MacAllister Architects," a woman said cheer-fully. "May I help you?"

"Ryan Sharpe, please," Carolyn said, drum-ming the fingers of one hand on the top of the desk.

"One moment, please, and I'll connect you."

"A thousand one, a thousand two," Carolyn muttered, "a thousand—"

"Ryan Sharpe."

Oh, my, Carolyn thought. She didn't remember Ryan's voice being quite that deep, quite that rum-bly, quite that…male and…

"Hello?"

"Yes," Carolyn said, much too loudly. "I mean, Ryan? This is Carolyn St. John. You have *got* to stop sending flowers to me. I mean, they're really lovely and it smells heavenly in here, but my office is starting to look like a garden or a funeral parlor.

"Not only that but the staff is having a field day trying to figure out who my romantic— That is, who is sending them and… It's very disruptive to our routine. So just stop it."

"Okay," Ryan said.

Carolyn frowned. "That's it? Okay? No plead-ing your case? Nothing?"

"Nope. I'll stop sending the flowers as soon as you agree to have lunch with me."

"That's blackmail, Ryan Sharpe," Carolyn said, smacking the desktop with the palm of her hand.

"Whatever works. Lunch? Today? I'll come by your office and pick you up."

"Don't you dare," Carolyn said, stiffening in her chair. "Everyone here will go bonkers if they can put a face with the flowers. No, no, no."

"Then I'll meet you wherever you say. Noon." Ryan paused. "There's a deli around the corner from your building that makes great subs, if you're open to suggestions."

No, not that deli, Carolyn thought. She'd gone there once, and the popular restaurant was so crowded and noisy that her hearing aids had shrilled painfully in her ears.

Oh, drat, she didn't want to have lunch with Ryan. She didn't want to even see the man again. The continuous stream of beautiful flowers had caused him to take front row center in her mind and follow her into her dreams at night. He was driving her crazy.

Well, there was only one way to end his ridiculous performance. Suffer through one lunch with him and that would be that. Fine. No, it wasn't, but what choice did she have?

"Carolyn?"

"Yes, all right," she said, sighing. "But not the deli. There's a small restaurant that's fashioned after an English pub in the next block. I can't remember the name of it but..."

"I know the place. Nice choice. It's very cozy, rather...intimate, shall we say. I'll see you there at noon sharp. 'Bye."

"Goodbye," Carolyn said, then her shoulders slumped with defeat as she replaced the receiver.

At exactly one minute before noon, Carolyn stood outside the intricately carved wooden door of the quaint little restaurant, and mentally pleaded with the butterflies to stop their frenzied flight in her stomach.

She wished she'd worn something more flattering today, she thought suddenly. Her gray suit with the pink blouse was very professional, she supposed, but she'd had it for several years, and the cut of the jacket was out of style and borderline frumpy.

Oh, for Pete's sake, what difference did it make? This wasn't a lunch date where she was attempting to impress. She'd been blackmailed into this meeting, a fact she was still angry about.

So why was she so shaken up about seeing Ryan Sharpe again? Oh, forget it. There was no point in asking herself a question she didn't know the answer to.

"Get a grip," she ordered herself, then squared her shoulders, lifted her chin and entered the restaurant.

She stopped immediately to allow her eyes to adjust from the bright sunlight to the rather dim, rosy glow created by candles burning on each of the small, cloth-covered tables. A smiling man in a suit and tie suddenly appeared before her.

"Ms. St. John?" he said, complete with a crisp, British accent.

"Yes, but how did you know that I'm..."

"Your gentleman told me that a lovely woman with dark hair, and eyes the color of a summer sky would be joining him," the man said. "You most definitely fit that description, madam."

"I do?" Carolyn smiled. "Well, fancy that." She frowned in the next instant. "What I mean is, yes, I'm Ms. St. John and I'm rather pressed for time, so if Mr. Sharpe has already arrived would you be so kind as to show me to his table...sir?"

"Of course. If you'll follow me, please?"

Forget it, buster, Carolyn thought. The butterflies had now doubled in number, her knees were trembling and... She did *not* want to be here. She did *not* want to see Ryan Sharpe again. She did *not* want...

"Madam?" the man said, from several feet away.

"Oh. Yes," Carolyn said, starting forward. "Certainly."

As Carolyn followed the ever-so-proper man, she saw Ryan seated at a table in the distance. Her heart quickened as he smiled and got to his feet.

How strange, Carolyn thought rather dreamily. The butterflies had zoomed out of her stomach and fluttered down to create a magic carpet that was floating her toward Ryan, because she surely wasn't doing anything so mundane as putting one foot in front of the other. Oh, no, not when Ryan was smiling that smile and gazing at her with those mesmerizing obsidian eyes of his.

"Hello, Carolyn," Ryan said quietly, when she reached the table.

Hello, who? she thought foggily, then blinked.

"Yes. Well, hello, Ryan," she said, tearing her gaze from his.

The man assisted her with her chair and she sank onto it gratefully, her trembling legs threatening to give way beneath her. She spread her napkin on her lap, smoothed it, then straightened the corners into a perfect square.

"I'm very glad to see you again," Ryan said. "Thank you for coming, for having lunch with me."

He was *more* than glad to see her, he thought. As he'd watched her come closer and closer to him

he'd been consumed by a strange sense of...
rightness, of her being where she belonged...with
him. A warmth had crept around his heart, then,
an instant later, coiled and churned low in his body
as desire flared into flames of heat.

His intense reaction to Carolyn was unexpected,
but here it was, and for reasons he couldn't begin
to fathom he welcomed it, embraced it, owned it
willingly.

Carolyn slowly raised her head, looked directly
at Ryan, ignored the pitter-patter of her heart and
prayed to the heavens that she didn't have a dopey,
dreamy expression on her face.

"Let's order our lunch, shall we?" she said. Oh,
good grief, was that *her* voice, that I-can-hardly-
breathe-when-I'm-this-close-to-you sound? "My
desk is stacked with work. Said desk that will no
longer hold flower vases because I'm here as
agreed."

"You're dusting me off." Ryan frowned.
"Won't you accept my apology for my earlier behavior? Give me another chance?"

Carolyn sighed. "So you can get on your soap-
box? Ryan, you believe that bringing Asian children here is basically wrong because they don't
resemble their adoptive families or their peers. You
feel that what I do, what I'm devoted to doing is

right…only to a point. I don't want to hear all that again.''

"I'm very sorry about what I said that day. Please, Carolyn, believe that. I'm extremely grateful for my loving family and the advantages I've had.

"Yes, I had some problems, but that's no excuse for saying what I did to you, and I know that. Let's start all over again. Okay? Have dinner with me tomorrow night? It will be Friday, the beginning of the weekend, a new beginning for us that can erase what happened in your office the other day. Please?''

Nope, Carolyn thought, deciding that her napkin needed attention again. She was *not* going out to dinner with Ryan. No way.

Then again… It had been months since she'd been on a date. Months. Ryan was charming, intelligent, so handsome it was ridiculous, and he *had* apologized about a gazillion times for the crummy, negative things he'd said that first day and…

It would be a nice change to go out on a Friday night, instead of spending another one curled up with a good book. Not that she didn't like to read good books, but… Was she mentally babbling? Yes, she was, no doubt about it, due to the fact that Ryan Sharpe had the capability of throwing her off-kilter. But as long as she was aware of that fact, she could stay one step ahead of it, or ignore it, or whatever and...

"All right," she said, looking at Ryan again. "I'll have dinner with you tomorrow night, Ryan."

"You will?" Ryan said, an incredulous tone to his voice.

"Yes."

"Great. Fantastic. Seven o'clock? I'll need your address, too. For the record, I want you to know that I was fully prepared to resume my flower crusade to get you to agree to dinner."

"Oh, spare me." Carolyn laughed. "The flowers were lovely, really beautiful, but the whole staff at the agency was hovering around, trying to get me to divulge who my admirer was." Her smile faded. "I really don't care for being the center of attention like that. It makes me uncomfortable."

"Uh-oh. Do I owe you another apology for sending all those flowers."

"No," she said, smiling at him warmly. "I've never had flowers delivered to me before. Not once in my life. They really were beautiful and...well, thank you."

"You've never received a bouquet of flowers from a man?" Ryan frowned.

"Are you folks ready to order?" a waitress said, appearing at the table.

"Yes," Carolyn said quickly.

Bless you, sweet lady, she thought. She didn't want to go further down this conversational path of poor little Carolyn St. John, who had never been the recipient of a bouquet of flowers from a man who had centered his thoughts on her.

"What would you like to eat?" Ryan said.

"I have no idea," Carolyn said, laughing, as she snatched the menu from the top of the table. "I'll only take a second to decide, though. I really do have so much work to tend to this afternoon."

"Fair enough." Ryan opened his own menu. "We can make this a quick lunch and follow it by a leisurely, unhurried dinner tomorrow night."

Yes, that was true, wasn't it? Carolyn thought, scanning the selection on the menu. And it sounded very, very nice.

Chapter Three

Carolyn hummed a peppy tune as she turned one way, then the other in front of the mirror hanging on the inside of her closet door.

Excellent, she thought. The dusty-rose, lightweight wool dress she'd purchased during her lunch hour seemed even more lovely now than it had in the store.

The long sleeves closed at her wrists with three small pearl buttons, and three matching buttons formed a delicate line down from the round collarless neckline. It was simple, but she hoped rather classy.

Her strappy, two-inch-heel evening sandals and small clutch purse were just the right finishing touch. Her hair was freshly shampooed, her makeup applied with exacting care and she'd added a dab of floral cologne.

She was ready.

To see Ryan.

To spend the next handful of hours with an incredibly handsome man, who had not been far from her thoughts the entire day as she anticipated their evening together.

Carolyn closed the closet door, then stared into space with a slight frown.

She was behaving ridiculously, she thought. Good grief, she'd skipped lunch so she could go shopping for a new dress, had rushed home to shower and shampoo her hair, had spent a silly amount of time getting her makeup just the way she wanted it and...

Carolyn smiled. "And I'm glad I did."

She snatched up the clutch purse from the bed, left the bedroom and went down the short hall to the living room where she set the purse on an end table.

She could tell herself, she supposed, that she'd gone to all this fuss and bother because this was her first date in many months and she deserved to go a bit overboard.

But that wouldn't be true.

She was giddy and acting rather out of character because she was going out with Ryan Sharpe. There. That was the truth. She should probably be unsettled by that realization, but she refused to do anything to dim her euphoric mood.

She was definitely not going to listen to the nagging little voice in her mind that kept whispering the fact that she was not convinced, despite Ryan's apologies, that he approved of her life's work. It was there, that doubt, hovering in the shadows and...

Oh, Carolyn, stop it. This date wasn't the beginning of anything of importance. It was just a night on the town with a dynamic man. She wasn't going to analyze her behavior or Ryan's attitudes to death, she was simply going to enjoy herself, feel pretty, special and feminine for a number of hours and that would be that.

"Go for it, Carolyn," she said merrily, then spun around as a knock sounded at the door. "There he is. Right on time."

Carolyn hurried to the door, opened it and made no attempt to curb her smile as she drank in the sight of Ryan Sharpe.

Yes, indeed, she thought, he was gorgeous. Dark-gray suit, black shirt, gray tie with a thin burgundy stripe and a burgundy handkerchief peeking above the edge of the pocket of his jacket. He looked as if he'd just stepped off the pages of a men's fashion magazine and he was here to collect *her* for a dinner date.

This was stuff of which fantasies were made, and she intended to enjoy every moment of the night ahead.

"Hello, Ryan," she said, stepping back. "Please come in."

He would, Ryan thought dryly, if he could remember what it took to walk, breathe, perform like a normal human being. His heart was thudding so fast in his chest he was probably having a heart attack and would pass out cold at this beautiful woman's feet.

She was exquisite.

He wanted to memorize every detail of her, then—oh, yeah—then pull her into his arms and kiss her until they were both weak with desire, need and...

"Ryan?"

"Hmm?" he said absently, then shook his head slightly. "Oh, yes." He entered the apartment, then turned to face Carolyn as she closed the door and met his gaze. "You look so lovely, so pretty in that dress that I wish I could think of better words than lovely and pretty."

"Well, thank you," she said, a flush warming her cheeks. "You're rather dashing yourself."

"I've been looking forward to our dinner date all day," Ryan went on.

"Really? Well, since you're being so forthcoming, I'll admit that I've had a sense of anticipation about it myself."

"Good, that's good." Ryan laughed. "I would have brought you flowers, but I thought I'd better cool it in that department for a while. I wouldn't want to trigger that temper of yours, Ms. St. John."

"Heaven forbid, Mr. Sharpe," she said, laughing with him.

"Shall we go? I made reservations." Ryan glanced around the medium-size living room and nodded. "I like your place. It's homey, warm and welcoming. This must be nice to come home to at the end of a busy day."

"Yes. Yes, it is." Carolyn cocked her head slightly to one side as she studied Ryan. "Isn't your home warm and welcoming?"

"Not really." He frowned. "I've never taken the time to do much more than buy and borrow the bare essentials of furniture with none of the touches that make four square walls into a home. But that's going to change. I've decided that this is the year I draw up the plans for a house, have it built and get out of that drab, boring apartment."

"How exciting. Was that your New Year's resolution?"

"One of them. We really should be on our way."

"You made more than one New Year's resolution?" Carolyn said as they left the apartment. "I forgot to make any, which is just as well because I either forget what they were or realize halfway through the year that I wasn't doing what I said I would. What else was on your list?"

"Oh, just this and that," Ryan said, as they left the building. "Are you hungry? The restaurant I picked has great food."

"I'm starved."

As Ryan assisted her into his vehicle, Carolyn's mind drifted back to the conversation they'd just shared about Ryan's New Year's resolutions. When she'd pressed him, he skittered away from the subject, had actually averted his eyes from hers at that moment.

Was that strange? she wondered. Oh, forget it. She wasn't going to clutter her mind with unimportant questions. She seriously doubted that Cinderella used mental energy pondering over mundane details while she was on measured time with the prince.

No, Cinderella had savored feeling special and beautiful and devoted her entire attention to the prince until it was time to end the evening. And that was exactly what *she* was going to do.

"Tell me about this house you're going to design for yourself," Carolyn said, as Ryan drove expertly through the busy traffic.

"I don't have anything etched in stone in my mind. I just know I want lots of space, big rooms with plenty of windows to allow the sun to come in from all directions."

"Have you considered a fireplace? When we get some of those winter rains, it's damp and chilly. Wouldn't a fireplace with warm, crackling flames be heavenly?"

"Sold," Ryan said, glancing over at her with a smile, then redirecting his attention to the traffic. "Add one fireplace. A flagstone fireplace, I think, banked by oak bookshelves that go all the way to the ceiling."

"Perfect. Oh, this is fun. I can certainly understand why you chose to become an architect. You make people's dreams for their special home come true. And this time, you're fulfilling your own dreams."

"Mmm," Ryan said.

Not really, sweet Carolyn, he thought. The home he'd dreamed about for many years would have the sound of happy children's laughter and the lilting voice of the woman he had married and pledged his love to for all time. But that was a forgotten dream.

During the hectic Christmas holidays, he'd managed to get in touch with himself and make some resolutions. As a step toward achieving some inner peace in regard to his heritage, he'd decided to remain single. He would date when he was attracted to someone. But he'd decided to watch and listen for any clues that might reveal that while a woman might enjoy his company, she certainly wouldn't want to marry and have mixed-heritage children with him.

Ah, hell, Sharpe, he admonished himself. Don't go there. Don't do anything to mar this evening with Carolyn. Just don't.

"A garden tub," Carolyn said, pulling him back to the subject at hand. "You know, one of those enormous, raised bathtubs that are big enough for two people and…"

Her voice trailed off as sudden images of her and Ryan in a garden tub filled with warm water flitted through her mental vision. They were naked…of course. And there were fragrant bubbles across the top of the water like frosting on a cake. Champagne. Oh, that was a nice touch. They were sipping champagne from wafer-thin tulip glasses as they sat close together, gazing into each other's eyes and…

Good grief, she thought, where was all this coming from? She didn't indulge in erotic daydreams, for Pete's sake.

"Then again," she said, hearing the thread of breathlessness in her voice, "I guess most men prefer showers over baths, don't they? Forget the garden tub."

"Oh, I don't know. That big tub you're describing holds a certain appeal, I must say. I could add an enclosed shower stall for when I wanted a quick in and out, and use the tub for really relaxing, unwinding from a long day."

"That works," Carolyn said, nodding, "but let's change the subject. I think it's rather nuts to be discussing styles of bathtubs, don't you?"

Not really, Ryan thought, because all kinds of decisions had to be made when designing a house. Discussing that garden tub, however, wasn't a terrific idea at the moment because the mental picture it was creating was kicking his libido into overdrive.

"There's the restaurant just up ahead," he said, extremely glad to see the familiar building. "We're shifting gears from bathtubs to delicious food."

And none too soon, Carolyn thought, willing her racing heart to return to a normal tempo.

The restaurant was one of Ventura's finest and most popular. Carolyn and Ryan were shown to a small table in one of the many charming alcoves, affording them enviable privacy.

They ordered from large menus edged in satin binding, Carolyn's menu had no prices printed on the parchment where the selections had been done in calligraphy. Ryan chose, tasted and approved a fine wine.

They chatted about the clever additions of the alcoves in the restaurant, moved on to the subject of the weather, then the winning record of a local basketball team made up of firefighters, police officers and members of the city counsel.

Crisp salads were placed in front of them, followed by Carolyn's order of baked salmon with dill sauce, and Ryan's choice of an enormous steak.

"Oh, this is all so delicious," Carolyn said. "I have a feeling I'm going to eat every bite."

"You're not alone in that. This steak is great." He paused. "So, tell me about Carolyn St. John, Ms. Carolyn St. John. How did you settle on a career involving international adoptions?"

"Is this going to lead to another argument on the subject?" she said, smiling, while telling the nagging voice in her mind to hush.

Ryan raised his right hand. "No, ma'am. I solemnly swear it is not. I'm attempting to get to know you better, and since your career is a very important part of who you are, it's a reasonable question. Okay?''

"Okay," she said, laughing. "Well, I grew up in Arizona and my parents still live in Phoenix. When I was a senior in high school there was a career day held and I spent quite a bit of time talking to a representative from an adoption agency. Something just clicked, and I knew that was what I wanted to do, be a part of.''

Ryan nodded.

"I went to Arizona State University and lived at home to save money. I have a bachelor degree in social work and another in human services. When I was close to graduating, I got on the Internet to see what jobs were available, found the agency here in Ventura, and as they say, the rest is history.''

"Interesting. You have two degrees?''

"It made sense at the time.'' Carolyn laughed. "Looking back I wonder how I did that, because it seemed I was always studying and never getting enough sleep.''

"Do you have brothers and sisters?''

"No,'' Carolyn said, redirecting her attention to her plate. "I'm an only child.''

Because special needs children require a great deal of time, energy and money to raise, she thought. Due to that her parents didn't have the big family they'd originally planned on, but continually assured her that she was so precious to them it didn't matter one iota.

"Did you have a happy childhood?"

"My goodness, I feel as though I'm being interviewed for a magazine article or something," Carolyn said, forcing a smile to her lips. "What about you? Do you have siblings?"

"An older sister." Ryan studied Carolyn for a moment as he caught the fact that she had avoided answering his question about her childhood. "It's a cool story. My father was a police officer and met my mom when she was newly divorced and very pregnant. He ended up delivering my sister himself before the ambulance crew got there. He considered Patty to be his daughter even before she was born."

"Oh, that is so sweet, so romantic. And then later they adopted you?"

"Yeah," Ryan said, nodding. "My dad had mumps way back when and wasn't able to have kids. So...after a ton of paperwork and months of waiting, they flew to Korea and got me when I was six months old. End of story."

"But it really isn't, is it?" Carolyn said softly, looking directly at him. "You had a difficult time adjusting."

Ryan lifted one shoulder in a shrug. "Off and on. I think it was a bit rougher for me because I was half-Korean and half-American. But enough of this, unless you want me to rattle off a bunch of Korean for you. I took a class in the language before I made a trip to Korea about a year or so ago. I learned enough to get by over there, but I guess Korean spoken with an American accent sounds pretty weird, because I set off a bunch of people in fits of laughter at times when I was attempting to communicate with them."

"Did you enjoy your visit there?"

"No," Ryan said. "Are you going to have room for dessert? They have a Black Forest cake here that is sensational."

In other words, Carolyn mused, anything that touched on Ryan's heritage was closed.

The conversation shifted again as they finished their meal with Ryan explaining that the Sharpe family was considered to be official members of the large MacAllister clan.

"My dad and Ryan MacAllister were partners on the Ventura police force for many years before they retired. They named their sons after each other." Ryan laughed. "Which is why my name is Ryan in case you're not following all this. I have a bunch of cousins, aunts, uncles, a set of grandparents, the whole nine yards, who aren't really related to me but—'' He shrugged.

''But they love you and you love them,'' Carolyn said, smiling.

''Yes,'' Ryan said seriously. ''Yes, I love them all, very much. Believe me, Carolyn, I know how lucky, how blessed I am to have been adopted by Hannah and Ted Sharpe. I not only have wonderful parents and a super sister, but I'm part of the MacAllister family, too.''

Ryan pushed his plate to one side and folded his arms on the top of the table.

''I've upset and—and hurt a lot of fantastic people,'' he went on, ''by my inability to find an inner peace. Last year my grandfather, Robert Mac-Allister, gave me a special gift, a…well, that's another story.

''What I'm trying to say here is that my problems are mine, are within me, are certainly not caused by any lack of love showered on me by my family the entire time I was growing up.

''I'm working hard, very, very hard, at getting a grip on the whole thing. It's coming. Slowly, but it's coming…the peace, little by little.'' He drew a deep breath and let it out slowly. ''What I did, said, in your office, though, was a red alert to me that I have a ways to go yet. I really am terribly sorry about what happened that day. Seeing all those pictures of the adopted kids just triggered a lot of memories and... Ah, hell, there's no excuse for my behavior and I sincerely hope you've forgiven me.''

''Of course I have,'' Carolyn said, reaching across the table to cover his hand with one of hers as the nagging voice stilled. ''I understand so much better now why— Oh, Ryan, I hope so much that you find your peace, move past your feelings. I understand about being different and...'' Her voice trailed off.

Ryan frowned as he laid his other hand on top of Carolyn's where it rested on his.

''What do you mean?'' he asked.

''Oh, well,'' she said, attempting to pull her hand free. Ryan tightened his hold, keeping her hand firmly in place between his. ''I...my career. Yes. I help create families that are a mixture of cultures. I'm confident at the time a child is placed with the new parents that all is well in that arena, but sometimes there are doubts, a problem or two with the extended family...

''You know, grandparents who might have difficulty accepting this foreign child as their grandchild. I work with those people as much as possible so that the child will know he or she, is totally loved and that...um...being different really isn't important, doesn't matter, and—'' She cleared her throat. "I'm going to be sinfully indulgent and have some Black Forest cake."

Ryan stared intently at Carolyn, then released her hand when she tugged on it again.

Something isn't right here, he thought. Carolyn had been scrambling for an explanation about what she had said about knowing what it was like to be different. She'd started talking too fast, had been nearly babbling with her dissertation about unaccepting grandparents or whatever. The color had drained from her face, too, and she hadn't looked directly at him while delivering her sermonette in a voice that was trembling slightly.

Ah, Carolyn, Ryan thought, what's going on here? What *wasn't* she telling him? What secrets did she have that she didn't trust him with? Yet.

Carolyn leaned back in her chair and produced a small smile.

"Enough heavy discussions," she said. "Are you going to have some cake with me?"

"Sure," Ryan said, signaling to the waiter. "Would you like coffee with it?"

"No, thank you. The water in my goblet will be fine. Maybe we won't feel so guilty about being piggy and having Black Forest cake if we both eat it. You know, like partners in crime, or something."

Ryan smiled. "There you go."

The tension of what had just transpired dissipated when the gooey, cherry-smothered pieces of cake were set in front of them. The tension was gone...but not forgotten.

When they were driving away from the restaurant, Carolyn asked Ryan if he knew where he was going to build his dream home.

Ryan nodded. "I have a piece of land that was given to me by my parents on my twenty-first birthday. It's a Sharpe family tradition to be given a piece of undeveloped property on the big twenty-one. We can sell it, keep it, build a home on it, whatever suits our fancy."

"How marvelous. And you like the location of your land?"

"Oh, yeah," Ryan said, nodding. "It's on a rise and has an unbelievable view of the city lights." He paused. "Would you like to see it? We could drive up there right now in this vehicle, even though there aren't any paved roads leading to it yet."

Ryan laughed. "There's a new one for you. Instead of asking if you want to see my etchings, I'm suggesting that you look at a bunch of dirt and scrub weeds with me. Classy, huh?"

"To the max," Carolyn said, smiling, "but I'd enjoy it, I'm sure."

"Okay. We're heading for the hills."

* * *

Twenty minutes later, after a drive that slowly left the city behind and gradually gained altitude as Ryan wove his way upward, he stopped and turned off the ignition to the SUV.

He crossed his arms on top of the steering wheel and swept his gaze over the fantastic view of the city lights that spread out below as far as the eye could see in all directions. He looked over at Carolyn, who had undone her seat belt and was leaning forward.

"What do you think?" he said.

"It's breathtaking," Carolyn said, awe ringing in her voice. "Oh, Ryan, what an incredibly beautiful view this is. I could sit here for hours and just drink in the sight of it. It's so perfect it looks like a postcard."

"Mmm," Ryan said, nodding. "Yes, it does, now that you mention it. Would you like to get out so you can see it firsthand instead of through the window?"

"I thought you'd never ask." Carolyn laughed as she opened the door and slid off the seat.

They met in front of the vehicle, and Carolyn wrapped her hands around her elbows as a chilly breeze caused her to shiver.

"It's windier up here than down in the city. This

isn't such a hot idea, Carolyn. You're obviously getting cold.''

"Oh, a few minutes won't hurt," she said, then shivered again.

Ryan stepped behind her and encircled her with his arms, stepping close to nestle her to him. Carolyn stiffened for a moment, then relaxed, savoring the warmth of Ryan's massive, powerful body.

Oh, he was so strong yet so gentle, she mused. She was definitely not cold any longer. The heat emanating from Ryan was suffusing her, swirling inside her, causing her heart to quicken its tempo. That heat was growing hotter, beginning to burn within her with licking flames of desire.

Move away, Carolyn, she ordered herself. This was dangerous, was too intimate and... It was as though she and Ryan had been transported to another world where no one existed but the two of them. And in this world there were no rules of conduct that must be followed. They were free to do whatever felt right and real, theirs.

Oh, yes, she had to step forward, out of Ryan's embrace that was muddling her thinking, and she would. In a minute. Or two. Three at the very most.

"I think," Ryan said, his voice husky, "that I'd design the house so that there was a big deck in the back, here, so I could sit in a lounge chair and enjoy this view whenever I wanted to. What do you think?''

I think my bones are dissolving, Carolyn thought. She really was going to end this unbelievably romantic moment and replant her behind safely on the seat in Ryan's vehicle. She certainly was. In…just…a…few…minutes, give or take a couple.

''That sounds like a great idea,'' she said, ignoring the weird trembling of her voice. ''Right up there on the top of the list with the fireplace and the garden tub.''

''Oh, man, Carolyn, you feel so good in my arms. You smell like flowers, do you know that? You hair is so silky, so…''

''Ryan…''

He shifted from where he stood to stand in front of her without totally releasing his hold on her. In the silvery glow of the millions of stars in the heavens their gazes met. Of their own volition, it seemed, Carolyn's hands floated from where they still cupped her elbows to encircle Ryan's neck.

And then he lowered his head and kissed her.

Oh, my, Carolyn thought.

Oh, yes, Ryan thought.

The kiss was tentative at first, then deepened, as Ryan parted Carolyn's lips and slipped his tongue into the sweet darkness of her mouth that held the lingering flavors of chocolate and cherries.

Hearts beat in wild tempo, and heat licked throughout them. Flames threatened to consume them with an intensity of want and need neither had experienced before.

Ryan lifted his head slightly to draw a quick, sharp breath, then tilted his mouth in the opposite direction and claimed Carolyn's lips once again.

Slow down, Sharpe, Ryan thought suddenly. He was losing control, was close to the edge. He had to stop kissing Carolyn now…right now. But, oh, man, how he wanted her. She was responding to him in total abandon, giving as she received. But he didn't want to do anything to frighten her, cause her to refuse to see him again. He had to get a grip.

Damn it, Sharpe, let go of her.

Ryan broke the kiss, grasped Carolyn's shoulders and eased her away from his throbbing, aroused body. She blinked several times, then drew a steadying breath.

"My…goodness," she managed to say, with a little puff of air.

"No joke," Ryan said, taking a step backward. He dragged one hand through his hair to keep from reaching for her again. "I think…we'd better go before— If I kiss you again I'm afraid I'll..." He pointed to the SUV. "Get in the vehicle."

A bubble of laughter escaped from Carolyn's lips. "Do you want me to salute first, now that you're barking orders at me?"

Ryan smiled, then drew one thumb over the soft skin of her cheek, causing a frisson of heat to slither down her back.

"Ah, Carolyn," he said, "you are so special. I like being with you more than I can say." He chuckled. "I don't exactly hate kissing you, either, but I don't think I can handle a long discussion about that part at the moment. Come on. I'll take you home."

Carolyn matched his smile and nodded. Ryan encircled her shoulders with one arm to lead her to the vehicle, but she hesitated, turning her head to look once more at the gorgeous view of the city lights below, etching it indelibly in her mind.

"Thank you for sharing this with me, Ryan."

"Sure," he said, as they started forward.

Except, maybe it had been a mistake to bring Carolyn up here, he thought, frowning. This was the place where he'd hoped and prayed he'd obtain the inner peace he sought.

But now? Carolyn had been here. Carolyn had shared kisses so incredibly passionate with him here. Carolyn's image might hover here, haunt him in the future, make him ache with the want of her, emphasize his aloneness. His loneliness.

Knock it off, he told himself, as he assisted Carolyn onto the seat and closed the door. Why go looking for trouble that wasn't even a reality? So he'd brought a lovely woman to his land, and they'd shared a couple of kisses under the stars. It wasn't *that* big of a deal.

Was it?

Chapter Four

Late the next afternoon, Carolyn stifled a yawn as she and Ryan peered at a display of green peppers at the outdoor farmers' market where they were shopping.

She glanced at Ryan to be certain he hadn't noticed, that like a sleepy toddler, she was very much in need of a rejuvenating nap, and was relieved to see that he was concentrating on the vegetables.

Being out in the fresh air, Carolyn mused, combined with the fact that she hadn't slept well the previous night had caused the yawn to nearly escape from her lips. No, she hadn't slept well because she had been consumed with thoughts and... yes, with desire.

For Ryan.

When he'd kissed her good-night just inside her door last night she'd come unsettlingly close to asking him if he wanted to stay, if he wanted to make love with her. She'd been so shocked by her own wanton yearnings that she'd stiffened in Ryan's arms, causing him to release her and step backward.

He'd said something she couldn't totally remember about being glad that one of them was keeping a cool head, or some such thing, then invited her to go to the farmers' market the next afternoon.

Their outing included the fact, he'd added, that he would cook a scrumptious omelet for their dinner with the fresh produce. Did that sound like something she'd enjoy doing with him? She'd bobbed her head up and down like one of those silly gizmos that people put on their dashboards, then before she could draw enough air into her lungs to speak, Ryan had left her standing there, closing the door behind him with a click.

And then she'd tossed and turned through the long hours of the night, getting only snatches of sleep. She'd done her usual Saturday chores of cleaning the apartment and washing clothes, and was very much in need of a snooze when Ryan picked her up at three o'clock.

But given a choice between taking a nap and being here with Ryan? Carolyn thought, sliding another glance at him. No contest. She was having such fun. She was with Ryan. He was very serious about veggies, that was for sure, and she was continually bursting into delighted laughter as he scrutinized all and everything before making his selections for the promised omelet.

"Mmm," Ryan said, holding a green pepper in each hand and narrowing his eyes. "Each of these little green guys has something going for it, but..." He nodded and put one back on the pile. "This is the one."

"You're sure?" Carolyn smiled. "This is not a lightweight decision you're making here, Ryan. You rejected at least forty-two scallions before you found exactly the right ones. You've only looked at about ten of those peppers."

"Trust me. I know my peppers, ma'am. The one that I chose is perfection personified."

"Yes, sir. Whatever you say, sir," she said, laughing again.

As Ryan paid for the pepper, then added it to the other purchases, Carolyn made no attempt to hide her smile that was determined to remain firmly in place.

She felt so young and carefree, she thought, was having such a wonderful time. She couldn't remember when she'd laughed right out loud so much. Ryan was turning a simple thing like shopping for vegetables into a memory-making adventure.

He was fun and funny, attentive, was making her feel, once again, important and special, feminine and pretty. They were each wearing jeans and sweaters, but he'd said she looked lovely, and the very instant he'd said it, she'd *felt* lovely in her casual outfit.

She was with Ryan, and there was nowhere else she could even imagine wishing to be.

As Ryan looked into the bag he was holding to double-check what he'd purchased, Carolyn frowned. When they left the farmers' market, they would be going to Ryan's apartment where he would prepare their dinner. Ryan's apartment. Just the two of them. The door closed, shutting out the world beyond.

At some point, she knew, he would take her into his arms and kiss her, just as he'd done when he'd arrived at her place to pick her up. He would kiss her, hold her close, cause desire to churn within her with that incredible heat that was beginning to become familiar, despite being like nothing she'd experienced before. Before Ryan.

Oh, my, Carolyn thought, what was happening to her? It was as though everything connected to Ryan was moving in fast-forward, taking her into an emotional and physical arena where she rarely even went, let alone this quickly.

Ryan was casting a spell over her. No, that was ridiculously dramatic and an attempt to blame him for her out-of-character behavior. The reactions she was having to Ryan Sharpe were hers, and she had to own them, be responsible for her behavior.

She and Ryan, she mentally rambled on, as she fell in step beside him as he continued down the row of booths, had known each other such a short time. But it didn't seem short, for reasons she couldn't even begin to fathom. That she was even fantasizing about making love with him so soon was throwing her off-kilter.

But then again...the very thought of it in her mind, her heart, had such a rightness to it, a sense of what was meant to be.

Good grief, Carolyn thought, shaking her head, she was driving herself totally nuts. She had to stop thinking so much, just settle down and enjoy the time she was spending with Ryan.

Ryan Sharpe, who didn't even trust her enough to reveal his innermost secrets, the reasons he had had such a difficult time dealing with his heritage, with being different.

How could she even be considering making love
with a man who was keeping such an important
part of who he was out of her reach?

Reality check, Ms. St. John, she told herself. *She*
was guilty of doing exactly the same thing. She
wanted to share the most intimate act between a
man and a woman with Ryan and yet she had not
told him *her* secret, the cause of her feeling different her entire life. Ryan had no idea that she
wore double hearing aids, was physically impaired.

Oh, what a muddled mess.

Carolyn sighed and Ryan looked over at her.

"Is something wrong? That was a rather sad-
sounding sigh, Carolyn."

"No, no, nothing is wrong," she said, smiling
up at him. "That wasn't a sad sigh. It was…it was
a yawn that I was attempting to stifle. All this fresh
air is making me sleepy. And I'm getting hungry,
too. I'm envisioning that omelet you promised me,
and the image of it in my mind is making my
mouth water."

"Ah, well, it will be worth waiting for. Guar-
anteed." He paused and look in the bag again.
"We're all set. Let's head for the parking lot."

"Who taught you how to cook?" Carolyn said,
as they continued to walk.

"My mother and grandmother. They tried to interest me in cooking when I was in high school, but I wasn't having any of that girly stuff.

"After I'd been on my own for a few years, I got very tired of eating fast food or sticking something in the micro. So I doubled back and asked them to teach me the basics. I discovered I really enjoyed putting together a nice meal and continued to try new things on my own."

Carolyn laughed. "Good for you. I'm still at the fast-food and sticking-things-in-the-micro stage. Cooking really doesn't hold any appeal for me."

They stopped at Ryan's vehicle, he opened the passenger door for Carolyn and she slid onto the seat.

"Well, that's not a problem, since I *do* like to cook."

Carolyn looked at him, but in the next instant he shut the door.

What had Ryan meant by that? she wondered, as he put the bag of vegetables on the back seat, then walked around to the driver's side. He made it sound as though they were a couple dividing up the chores in their home.

Oh, Carolyn, stop it. There she went again, thinking things to death. It was just a casual remark on Ryan's part, nothing more, a comment he'd made in response to her statement that she didn't like to cook. Just shut up, Carolyn St. John.

As Ryan drove out of the parking lot and merged with the busy traffic he frowned.

Weird, he thought. What he'd said in response to Carolyn's declaration was nothing short of weird.

It had made sense to him when he'd said it. She didn't like to cook, he did, so they didn't have a problem on that score.

But now that he thought about it, it sounded like a statement that would be made by a man who was in a serious relationship with a woman, one in which they were together so much that sharing meals was a given, and who was going to prepare them was up for discussion.

He was *not* involved in a serious relationship with Carolyn St. John, nor did he intend to be in the future. His New Year's resolution was etched in stone.

But how he felt about Carolyn was different, somehow, from anything he'd known before. It was a mishmash of emotions. There was a feeling of rightness, a comfortable essence of being where he belonged, while at the same time being acutely aware of his growing desire for her that caused all his senses to be heightened.

Man, how he wanted her. Ending that kiss last night in her apartment, stepping back, then leaving her had been a tough road to go. He'd gotten very

little sleep as he'd tossed and turned, thinking
about Carolyn, aching for Carolyn St. John.

Why? Why her? Why was she capable of pushing his buttons like this? Sure, she was pretty, really lovely, in a wholesome, down-to-earth way,
but he'd certainly dated other attractive women,
none of whom were interested in a serious
relationship.

So why was Carolyn turning him inside out?

Maybe, Ryan mused on, and this was a dangerous thought, maybe his subconscious was hitting
on the fact that given Carolyn's work, she harbored
no prejudices. That meant she wouldn't hesitate to
marry a man of mixed heritage, pledge her love to
him for all time and have his children, *their* children, a part of him, a part of her.

Oh, whoa, Sharpe, he admonished himself. Forget that stuff. He wasn't buying into that program.
No way. If he let down his guard, put his resolution
on the shelf and ignored it, he would be headed
for heartbreak…again, and he wasn't going to do
it.

As for marrying? Ryan repeated in his belea-
guered mind. Talk about weird. He was thinking
about something that might, just might, flicker
through his mind after dating a woman for many
months. He hardly knew Carolyn, for Pete's sake.

Yes, he enjoyed being with her. Yes, he desired

her with an intensity that was becoming more difficult to control. Yes, she was like a breath of fresh air because she *wasn't* worldly and sophisticated.

But Carolyn also had secrets, things she seemed determined not to share with him. Secrets kept took a toll. Secrets kept created barriers, walls between two people. Secrets kept meant that trust, deep and meaningful trust, just wasn't there.

He had his secrets.

And Carolyn apparently had hers.

So be it.

Those secrets couldn't damage their *relationship* because they weren't *in* a relationship.

Good. Okay. He'd sorted that out. Everything was fine, just fine.

Then why did the realization that Carolyn didn't completely trust him cause a cold, painful fist to tighten in his gut? Why in the hell did that stark knowledge hurt so damn much?

"I need food," Ryan said. "My brain is depleted or something, must have nourishment so it can get back on the right track."

"What wrong track is it on, your poor unfortified brain?" Carolyn looked over at him.

"It's too confusing to discuss. Now, then, do you want toast with your omelet? You have a choice between whole wheat or sourdough bread."

"Wheat," Carolyn said. "Am I to be assigned

a task toward accomplishing this gourmet delight? You know, chop up something?''

"Nope. You'll sit at the table and talk to me while sipping a glass of wine as I do my culinary thing with an expertise that will awe you beyond words.''

"Do tell,'' she said, laughing.

"Yep. You are in for a treat, Ms. St. John.'' Ryan paused and chuckled. "When I was in Korea I went to a huge open market and found it very fascinating. I have to admit that I didn't know what a lot of the stuff they were offering even was.

"I was strolling along and came upon an elderly lady, who looked like she was about a hundred years old. She was in a heated debate, I presumed, about the price of something she wanted to buy. I sort of hung around to see how it would end up.''

"How fun. What happened?''

"The merchant finally threw up his hands in defeat, and the old lady smiled and nodded. She'd won, by golly. Then guess what? She picked up a huge, live turtle out of a crate, tucked it under her arm and off she went. I swear that turtle weighed more than she did. I considered following her home to see if I could sample some of the turtle soup she was obviously going to make, but decided I'd probably get arrested if I dogged her heels.''

"Oh, gross,'' Carolyn said. "I know that turtle

soup is an Asian favorite, but I never gave any thought to the poor turtle.''

Ryan laughed. ''I could tell you about some of the other things I saw in that market but I'm afraid you'll lose your appetite for my omelet.''

''It sounds as though you had a good time in Korea, Ryan, even though you said that you didn't.''

''No, I really didn't. There's my apartment building up ahead.''

He'd done it again, Carolyn thought, frowning. Ryan had changed the subject. She didn't know why, and the sad thing was that it appeared he had no intention of telling her.

When they entered Ryan's apartment on the sixth floor of the building, Carolyn swept her gaze over the living room, once, then twice.

''Takes a little getting used to, doesn't it? I told you I just sort of threw it together and that was that. What you see is furniture from the clan that they didn't want anymore.

''That chair over there is an antique. The strange black-and-chrome thing is from my cousin Trip's rebel days. Trip is now known as Alice, which is her real name. She's an accomplished artist. That painting on the wall is one of hers, the only thing I'll take with me to my house when I get it built.''

Carolyn crossed the room and looked at the lovely painting that showed a castle on a rise and a multitude of gorgeous flowers flowing down the hill.

"This is beautiful," she said. "Your cousin is very talented."

"Yes, she really is very gifted," Ryan said, nodding. "That's a rendition of the castle on the Island of Wilshire where she lives with her husband, who is in charge of the vineyards. My cousin, Maggie, lives on the island, too, and is married to the prince who will someday be the king of the island."

"Really? It sounds like a romantic fairy tale." Carolyn said. "I think I remember reading about the royal weddings in the newspaper months ago. Something about Ventura cousins marrying royal cousins? Right?"

"Yes," Ryan said. "Both Maggie and Alice are expecting babies, along with my cousins Emily and Jessica. The MacAllisters are doing the baby-boom bit. I think it's great. I like babies, kids of all ages, for that matter. They're fascinating people in small bodies."

"Well," Carolyn said, turning to smile at Ryan, "you should have a half dozen or so of your own, then."

"No. Not me. Nope. Isn't going to happen." Ryan turned and headed across the room. "Standing here talking won't get us fed. Follow me, ma'am, so you can pick a good seat to watch a genius at work.''

Did that make sense? Carolyn thought, as she followed Ryan. One minute he was raving on about how much he liked babies, and the next thing she heard was a very adamant statement that he wasn't going to have any children, by golly. *Very* adamant. Why?

Did it have to do with the problems Ryan had encountered growing up? Had he been hurt so deeply that he had no intention of bringing his own mixed-blood children into the world? Oh, she hated the idea that Ryan had suffered pain of that magnitude. But maybe there was another reason he didn't want to be a father.

So many questions were beginning to pile up, none of which had answers. They were, she had a feeling, tangled in the web of the secrets Ryan refused to share with her.

Well, Carolyn thought, she wasn't going to dwell on any of that now. She was about to witness the creation of the omelet of the century, which deserved her undivided attention.

As Ryan had promised, Carolyn was soon seated at the kitchen table with a glass of wine while he proceeded to chop the various vegetables he'd purchased into tiny pieces.

They chatted about his cousins, with Ryan adding details of how beautiful the island of Wilshire was. Then Ryan related a hilarious tale of when he was six years old and had been determined to stay awake on Christmas Eve to see Santa Claus up close and personal.

"Did you see him?" Carolyn asked, smiling.

"Well, my folks went to bed," he said, as he dropped a handful of cut vegetables into a frying pan, "figuring I'd fall asleep in front of the fireplace and they could scoop me up later and put me in bed. I waited and waited, then finally decided it would be better to see the arrival of the sleigh on the roof."

"Uh-oh." Carolyn laughed.

"No joke. I sneaked out the front door, dragged a ladder from the garage and started climbing. There was an elderly man who lived across the street who didn't sleep much, nor could he see too well. He saw shadows, I guess, of someone trying to break into the Sharpe house by using a ladder to get in an upper window, and he telephoned the police, which was pretty dumb when you consider that my dad was a cop."

"What happened?"

"I'd just made it up onto the roof when the patrol cars arrived with lights flashing and sirens wailing." Ryan chuckled. "What a scene. My dad told me later that it was months before the other cops quit kidding him about the fact that he'd been snoozing away while a mean, lean crook was attempting to break into his house.''

''Was your father angry at you?''

''Well, both my dad and mom were scared silly when they thought about what could have happened if I'd fallen off the roof, but when my dad started to lecture me, my mom just came apart laughing and that was the end of it.

''Patty informed me that I was the dumbest brother she'd ever had, forgetting in her fury that I was the *only* brother she had ever had. That was a Christmas I will never forget,'' Ryan added the egg mixture to the pan of vegetables.

''Oh, my, what a marvelous story,'' Carolyn said. ''Your family sounds wonderful, Ryan.''

He nodded. ''They are. They really are.''

Carolyn hesitated a moment before speaking again, wondering if she dare make a comment about Ryan's childhood in general.

Nothing ventured, nothing gained, she decided.

''I imagine you have endless stories like that, such fond memories of your childhood,'' she said, looking intently at Ryan.

''Nothing in this world is perfect, Carolyn,'' he said quietly. ''Yes, I have nice memories, but I also have things I wish I could forget. Standing apart from everyone around you can be a lonely place to exist in.''

''Yes, I know,'' she whispered.

Ryan turned from where he was standing in front of the stove.

''What do you mean, Carolyn? How do you know?''

''Oh. Well.'' Carolyn shifted her gaze to the wine glass, running one finger slowly around the top edge. ''You've made it clear that being half-Korean created problems for you, although you haven't shared specific details. I'm...I'm simply acknowledging the rather vague reference you made to it, that's all.''

No, Ryan thought, concentrating his attention on his cooking again, that was *not* all. Carolyn was definitely, *definitely,* keeping something from him about herself, her *own* childhood. Damn.

''Okay,'' Ryan said, forcing a lightness to his voice. ''Gear up. You are a minute away from ecstasy in the form of sampling an omelet created by the one and only Ryan Sharpe, madam. This will be an experience like no other, a happening, a major event in your life.''

So are you, Ryan Sharpe, Carolyn thought, smiling at him warmly as he put a plate in front of her. So are you.

Ryan bowed deeply. ''Your omelet, my sweet,''

he said, straightening again. "I will now stare at you while you take the first bite, so I don't miss any of your totally overwhelmed reaction."

"Oh, okay," Carolyn said, unable to keep from laughing. She picked up her fork, filled it, then very slowly put it in her mouth. "Mmm." She chewed, swallowed, then her eyes widened slightly. "Oh, this is scrumptious, absolutely fabulous."

"Knocks you out, doesn't it?" Ryan said, sitting opposite her with his own plate.

"And the chef is so humble, too," she said. "I don't recall Julia Child ever saying 'My stars, but I'm a marvelous cook.'"

"Well, she should have," Ryan said. "I mean, hey, if you're good, you're good." He winked. "And, sweetheart, I'm good."

"I think I'll pass on that comment," Carolyn said, her mind already wandering to a mental list of just what else Ryan was *good* at doing. "But I will definitely give my compliments to the chef."

"Thank you, thank you."

The dinner was delicious and Carolyn ate every bite, complimenting the chef several times on his expertise. She offered to help tidy the kitchen, but Ryan refused, saying he even had that part down to an art and could do it quicker on his own.

"Oh, my gracious," Carolyn said, sinking onto

the sofa after they left the sparkling clean kitchen, "I am stuffed. I don't think I'll eat another thing for a week. Thank you again, Ryan. It really was a superb meal."

"You're very welcome," he said, settling next to her. "It was fun to cook for someone other than myself. I haven't done that in a long time. I'll have to make my secret recipe for spaghetti sauce for you. It's so good it boggles my mind."

"Don't talk about food," she said, laughing. "I think I just gained five pounds as it is."

"Okay, I won't say another word about eating. Except...well, do you think you'd like to come to dinner again sometime and sample my spaghetti?"

Carolyn turned her head to look at him, not realizing until that moment that he was so close. She gazed into the fathomless depths of his compelling dark eyes and felt her breath catch at the same time her heart quickened.

"Yes," she said softly, "I think I'd like that very much. Sampling. Your spaghetti."

"Good," Ryan said, lowering his head toward hers. "That's good. Sampling is good in a multitude of arenas. Like...this one...for example."

Ryan's mouth melted over Carolyn's in a kiss that was much, much more than just a sample. He shifted to encircle her with his arms as Carolyn clasped her fingers behind his neck. The kiss intensified even more, and heated desire consumed them.

Ryan broke the kiss only long enough to draw a rough breath, then claimed Carolyn's lips once again. Reality and reason began to fade into a sensuous mist that surrounded them, leaving only want and need.

Oh, how she wanted to make love with Ryan Sharpe. How could something that felt so very, very right be wrong?

Secrets, whispered a niggling little voice in her mind. How could either of them give of themselves completely when there were so many secrets standing between them?

Carolyn slowly and reluctantly slid her hands from Ryan's neck and flattened them on his chest, pressing gently. He released her instantly, his breathing labored.

"I want you," he said, his voice gritty with passion. "You know that. And I believe you want me every bit as much."

"Yes, but..."

"But," he interrupted, "if this isn't the time, isn't right for you, then it isn't going to happen. It's too important, Carolyn. We have to both be in the same place about this. Okay?"

"Yes. Okay. Thank you, Ryan."

Ryan took a deep breath, let it out slowly, then

smiled. "You are one very potent lady, Ms. St. John. I think I'm in for a long night of tossing and turning."

"Me, too, Ryan," she said, managing to produce a small smile.

"Listen, I promised to have dinner with my grandparents tomorrow evening, but could I see you Monday night?"

"Monday? No, I'm sorry but I'm busy on Monday night."

Ryan waited a beat to see if Carolyn would reveal her plans for Monday, but she said nothing.

"Okay, then, how about Tuesday?" he asked. Another secret? What was she doing on Monday night that she obviously didn't intend to share with him? "A new pizza place just opened up near here. Want to check it out with me?"

"Yes, that would be fun."

"It's a date. Tuesday. Pizza. I'll pick you up at your apartment at six-thirty. Work for you?"

Carolyn nodded. "Perfect."

"As for this point in time, my sweet…want to watch a movie?"

"Well, sure, that sounds fine."

"Great. We'll find a dandy flick on the movie channel." Ryan got to his feet. "But first I have some more kitchen duty to tend to."

"You do?" Carolyn said, frowning slightly.

"Indeed I do." He strode across the room. "Popcorn. It's against the law to watch a movie without consuming great quantities of hot, buttered popcorn."

"Oh-h-h," Carolyn said, wrapping her arms around her stomach, while moaning and laughing at the same time. "Don't fix any for me. I couldn't possibly eat another bite of anything tonight."

"You'll change your mind," Ryan yelled from the kitchen. "This is no ordinary buttered popcorn I'm about to prepare. This is one of my specialties. Trust me."

Trust me, Carolyn's mind echoed. She did trust Ryan, knew that trust was growing stronger with each passing moment they spent together.

But hovering there in the shadows, she thought gloomily, threatening that new and fragile trust, were the secrets they both were keeping.

Chapter Five

On Monday evening, Carolyn entered a large room at the community center and swept her gaze over the two dozen people who were gathered there. Some children were playing with a variety of toys, while others sat at a table, coloring pictures. There were as many adults as there were little ones, and Carolyn smiled as she realized there were more present than the week before.

Word was reaching those who needed to know, she thought, that free sign language classes were offered here on Monday nights for those unable to pay the fees of a private instructor.

Oh, what a difference it was going to make in the lives of these families to be able to communicate in their home with their hearing-impaired child. And for that child to have a means to interact with his or her peers in a school classroom where others talked with flying fingers.

"Okay, moms and dads," a woman in her fifties said, as she clapped her hands. "It's time to begin class. Those of you who have been assigned an instructor are all set. Folks here for the first time this evening should gather here by me."

In a flurry of activity people did as they had been told and Carolyn was approached by Mary, a woman in her late twenties and her six-year-old daughter, Kendra.

Carolyn smiled, then moved her hands and fingers as she spoke slowly to Kendra.

"Hello...Kendra," Carolyn spoke and signed. "How...are ...you...tonight?"

Kendra hesitated, then carefully moved her fingers. "Fine," she said, her voice having a flat, nasal sound.

"And you, Mary?" Carolyn said, and signed to Kendra's mother.

"Fine, thank you." Mary concentrated on the motions of her fingers, then dropped her hands to her sides. "We've been practicing our sign language at home all week. Kendra was able to tell me what she wanted for breakfast this morning by signing instead of pointing to things. Oh, Carolyn, I can't believe the progress she's made already. She's very excited about it, too.''

"Wonderful," Carolyn said, smiling. "Let's get seated and start to work, shall we?"

For the next hour the trio focused on learning several new words in sign language, Carolyn often bending fingers with a gentle touch to the proper position.

"Time...for...a...snack," Carolyn said and signed to Kendra.

Kendra nodded, slid off her chair and dashed across the room to where refreshments were set up.

"She's coming along beautifully, Mary," Carolyn said, "and you're to be commended for working with her so much at home." She paused. "Has her father come around at all on the subject of sign language?"

Mary sighed. "No. Jerry said he's not going to make a public spectacle of himself when he has Kendra on his visitation days by playing finger games as he calls it. He says they do just fine with her pointing at what she wants, or nodding or shaking her head. He isn't going to budge on the subject, Carolyn. I spoke to my divorce attorney and she says we can't force Jerry to take these classes.''

Carolyn frowned. "All we can do is hope he'll change his mind as time goes by."

"If he could only see how happy Kendra is when she realizes that she's being understood by signing. I've tried to tell Jerry what a difference it's making in her self-confidence, but he won't listen. He needs to witness it for himself." Mary laughed. "You know, like *show* and tell, not just me telling him, which he considers nagging on my part and tunes me out."

"Show and tell," Carolyn repeated, her mind racing as a sudden image of Ryan flashed before her mental vision, "instead of just telling. I wonder..." Her voice trailed off. "Maybe, just maybe... Well, it's certainly worth a try."

The next evening Carolyn paced restlessly around her living room as she waited for Ryan to pick her up to go to the new pizza place for dinner.

She was a nervous wreck, she admitted to herself. Everything was in place for her to carry out her plan and she was getting cold feet at the last minute. What if Ryan realized what she had done and became angry, felt she'd intruded into his private space? He might become so furious that he'd storm off and she'd never see him again.

Good grief, what an absolutely depressing thought.

Forget her sneaky plan. She wasn't going to do this.

But then again...show-and-tell.

A knock sounded at the door, and Carolyn gasped at the sudden noise.

"Get it together," she told herself, smoothing her red sweater over her jeans-clad hips. "In for a penny, in for a pound. I'm going to do it."

She opened the door and forced a smile onto her face. "Hello, Ryan," she said. "Come in."

Ryan was also wearing jeans with a sweater, but his sweater was a russet color which, Carolyn decided, suited him well.

"Hi," he said, entering the apartment. He dropped a quick kiss on Carolyn's lips. "Ready for some grand-opening pizza?"

"Yes, I am," she said. Courage, Ms. St. John. Deliver your spiel. Now. "However, if you don't mind, I need to make a quick stop before we go to eat."

"Sure. Where?"

"Where?" Carolyn said. "Oh, it's only a couple of blocks out of our way. I need to pop in for the last visit with one of my families so I can close their file. Pop in, pop out. That's it. Okay?"

Ryan shrugged. "No problem. Do they know you're coming?"

"Yes," Carolyn said. "I spoke with them this

afternoon and told them a friend would be with me on our way to dinner. This is just a routine wrap-up, show-and-tell thing.''

Ryan frowned. ''Show and tell?''

''Ignore that part,'' Carolyn said, snatching her purse from the sofa. ''Let's go.''

''Are you all right?'' Ryan said, following her out the door. ''You seem a tad wired.''

''Just hungry. Yes. I am really hungry. So, we'll do our pop-in, pop-out deal, then be on our way to get piggy with pizza. Right?''

''Right,'' Ryan said, eyeing her warily.

Carolyn gave Ryan directions, and they soon pulled into the driveway of a medium-size ranch-style home. It was painted robin's-egg blue, trimmed in white and had a perfectly manicured yard.

A smiling woman in her mid-thirties who was at least six feet tall answered Carolyn's knock.

''Come in, come in,'' the woman said. ''It's good to see you, Carolyn, and you must be Ryan. I understand you're checking out the new pizza place once you leave here.''

''That's the plan,'' Ryan said.

''Ryan,'' Carolyn said, once they were in the spacious living room, ''this is Sally Foster.''

''Oh, and here is my husband and daughter to greet you,'' Sally said. ''Chet, you know Carolyn, of course, and this is her friend, Ryan. That bundle Chet is carrying is our precious Elizabeth.''

Ryan stared at the man carrying an Asian baby girl who appeared to be close to a year old. The man was no more than five-eight, if that much. Ryan looked at Sally again, then back at Chet.

Whatever, Ryan thought. The differences in their height was unusual, that's all. No one would blink an eye if it was reversed, but it was out of the ordinary for a wife to be so much taller than her husband. But...whatever.

"Please, sit down," Sally said. "Would you like something to drink?"

"No, thank you," Carolyn said, sinking gratefully onto the sofa as her frazzled nerves created trembling legs. "We're saving ourselves for the pizza." She paused. "Hello, Elizabeth. Oh, she's so beautiful. Look at all that silky dark hair."

"Isn't she fantastic," Chet said, as he sat down with Elizabeth on his lap. "She took her first steps today, Carolyn. You should have seen her. Two little steps, and she knew she'd done something special."

"She's Chinese, isn't she?" Ryan said.

"Yes," Chet said. "We went over to China, thanks to Carolyn and the agency, and got her." He laughed. "I did all right when we were sight-seeing, but Sally caused quite a stir, didn't you, honey?''

Sally laughed. ''Oh, heavens, it was a hoot. Some people just stared at me like I was a monster from the deep and others backed away, terrified or something because I was so tall. I'm considered tall here, so you can imagine what it was like in China.''

''Sally and I are used to getting second looks, because of the difference in our sizes. We've been married for fifteen years, plus went together all through high school and we're quite used to it.'' He chuckled. ''But I must admit that the reaction in China was a bit more than we're accustomed to.''

''And now you have a foreign child to draw further attention to you,'' Ryan said quietly.

''Yes, I suppose that's true. But Elizabeth will soon learn, as Sally and I did, that stares, double takes, what have you, are not important. What counts is what we're based on...love. Elizabeth is our daughter. We're a family. That's all that matters.''

''So,'' Carolyn said a bit too loudly as Ryan frowned. ''Everything is all right here? We can put your file in the happily-ever-after cabinet at the office?''

''You certainly can,'' Chet said.

"Except for the fact that Elizabeth is a daddy's girl." Sally smiled. "I'll do while Chet is at work, but the minute she sees him that's it for me. She wants her daddy and there's no discussing it, thank you very much."

"Don't complain, Sally," Carolyn said, laughing. "It gets you off diaper detail the entire evening."

"And the bubble-bath dunk that can only be done by Daddy. I sit out here with my feet up reading the newspaper. Ah, life is good. Carolyn, we're so happy we're silly. We have our daughter at long last, and we are so grateful to Hands across the Sea."

"May I ask you something?" Ryan said.

"Certainly," Sally said.

"You obviously know Elizabeth's likes and what have you very well, and you're relaxed with her, and she's at ease with the two of you. There's also the way you refer to her as your daughter. It's not forced or phony…it's real. You love her very much. I was just wondering how long Elizabeth has been with you? You know, when you went to China to get her."

This was it, Carolyn thought, feeling a knot tighten in her stomach. This was the real goods, the bottom-line show-and-tell.

"We've been home from China for ten days,"

Sally said. ''In fact, we're still suffering from the last dregs of jet lag.''

''Ten...days?'' Ryan said, an incredulous tone to his voice. ''Days? Not months? Days?''

''Time for pizza,'' Carolyn said, jumping to her feet. ''We've done our pop-in, pop-out visit and off we go. Have a lovely evening. 'Bye.''

The Foster family escorted Carolyn and Ryan to the door where Carolyn grabbed Ryan's arm and hustled him outside. Sally and Chet called a cheerful farewell, and Elizabeth babbled.

Carolyn hurried to Ryan's vehicle and got in on the passenger side, clicking her seat belt into place. She chewed on her bottom lip as she watched Ryan cross the front yard, stop and look back at the house, then continue on, his brows knitted in a frown.

They were several blocks away from the Fosters' home before Ryan spoke, the sudden sound of his voice causing a stressed Carolyn to jerk in her seat.

''The Fosters are an unusual couple,'' he said.

''Oh?'' Carolyn said, attempting for a lightness to her voice that didn't quite materialize. ''Because of their difference in height?''

''No, not that,'' he said, with an edge of impatience. ''I'm talking about the instantaneous bonding that has taken place between them and that baby. You can hear the pride in their voices when they talk about Elizabeth, see the love in their eyes, on their faces, when they look at her. They've only been back from China for ten days? That can't be how it generally works.''

"Yes, it does, Ryan. It really does. That's why I'm able to make the last home visit so soon after our families return home. Whatever the Fosters face in the future they'll do it together with a foundation of love so solid that nothing will be capable of even making the tiniest chip in it. Elizabeth is loved beyond measure. She truly is.''

Ryan's grip on the steering wheel tightened for a long moment, then he drew a shuddering breath.

"I've got to think about this, about what I just saw in that home,'' he said. "I don't want to talk about it anymore tonight.''

"Yes, all right.''

They drove in silence the remainder of the way to the restaurant, then Ryan pulled into the crowded parking lot.

"Wow,'' he said, "look at the crowd. Do you still want to take this on?''

"You bet,'' Carolyn said. "I'm starving, remember? Pizza, here we come.''

They were soon caught up in the bedlam within the building, where everyone was having a marvelous time and the pizza was delicious. The tension that had been a nearly palpable entity in Ryan's vehicle dissipated, and their smiles became genuine, their laughter real.

They were given helium-filled balloons to celebrate the grand opening, and Ryan insisted they keep them when they left and decided to window shop since the weather was so pleasant. It was fun. They strolled along the sidewalk clutching the strings of their balloons, and Carolyn dissolved in a fit of laughter when Ryan stopped and tied the string around her wrist so there would be no chance of it escaping from her grasp.

It was only later that Carolyn's mind flitted back to what had taken place at the Fosters. What was Ryan thinking, or had he decided to dismiss the entire episode as unimportant? Had her show-and-tell duplicity had an impact on him, or had he already dusted it off and forgotten it?

She didn't know, may never know, but she was glad she had done what she had. She'd tried to help Ryan conquer his inner demons a little by taking him to the Fosters, and the sense of rightness, of caring, followed her into her dreams.

On Friday afternoon Carolyn sat in her office and stared into space.

Here she was again, she thought, daydreaming

about Ryan Sharpe, reliving every moment shared with him during the past week.

On Wednesday evening they had gone to the movies, then Thursday night Ryan asked her to accompany him to various furniture stores in Ventura so he could begin looking at furniture for his new home. He'd started on the plans, he'd told her, and he was so zinged about the whole thing now, he thought it would be a kick to start mentally furnishing some of the rooms.

Once again she'd had such carefree fun. And once again it had been close to impossible to send Ryan on his way when the outings were over.

"I can't go on this way much longer," Carolyn said, sighing.

Tonight Ryan was helping a buddy paint a nursery for the soon-to-be-born baby boy he and his wife were expecting. The project had been delayed while the couple debated vigorously on the color. The mommy-to-be wanted mint green, the daddy insisted on royal blue. A compromise had finally been reached, and several gallons of pale-blue paint were waiting to be applied.

Carolyn got to her feet, moved to the front of her desk and began to pace back and forth.

Well, she thought dryly, hadn't that been fascinating? She'd just done a mental travelogue, or some such thing, of her week with Ryan. She'd relived some very special memories, but there was no denying the fact that she had also been avoiding two very important issues.

One. The MacAllisters and those considered to be MacAllisters like the Sharpes and sundry others, had decided that, since the weather was unseasonably warm for January, they would have a family barbecue. Tomorrow. And she was going with Ryan. To meet his huge family. And the very image of that in her mind was enough to bring on an instant nervous breakdown.

Two. The sexual tension between her and Ryan had grown to the point that it was nearly unbearable. Even when they were engaged in various activities that caused them to laugh and have fun, it was there, hovering near, taunting, tempting, demanding their attention.

How many more times could she bear to kiss Ryan good-night at her door? How many more nights spent alone in her bed, missing Ryan, aching to make love with Ryan Sharpe, could she endure?

None.

Carolyn stopped her trek and wrapped her hands around her elbows as a chill swept through her.

What if, she thought, when Ryan took her home from the barbecue tomorrow evening she made it clear that she wanted to make love with him? She'd never been so brazen before in her life, but she'd never desired anyone the way she did Ryan Sharpe.

What if Ryan said no, just flat out rejected her? She knew he desired her, knew he became aroused when they kissed and held each other, but what if he didn't want to take that final step and make love with her? What if he viewed that intimate act as taking what they were sharing to a level of importance where he had no intention of going?

The mere thought of Ryan rejecting her was more than she could bear. She would be so humiliated, so diminished, her sense of self, her womanliness shattered into a million pieces.

Was it worth the risk?

Carolyn drew a wobbly breath.

"Yes," she whispered.

She cared deeply for Ryan. She liked him more than she could express in words and she liked who *she* was when she was with him. She respected him and could tell from the way he treated her that he returned that emotion in kind. And they were consenting adults.

By golly, while they were still together she wanted to create as many memories to keep as she could. She wanted to make love with Ryan Sharpe.

"Yes," she said, lifting her chin.

"You have ESP?" Janice said, entering Carolyn's office.

"What?" Carolyn said, spinning around.

"I was about to ask you if you had time now to go over these dossiers before we send them to be translated into Chinese. You said yes before I got that far."

"Ah," Carolyn said, tapping one fingertip against her temple, "now you know my powers, Janice. I can read minds. Cool, huh?"

"Creepy." Janice laughed. "Let's go back to reality." She set the stack of papers on Carolyn's desk. "The sooner you check these six packets, the quicker they get translated and ready to send to Bejing. There are six baby girls in China waiting to be matched with these parents-to-be."

"I'll start on them right away."

"Okay, good." Janice started toward the office door. "Oh, and if you really can read minds? Don't peer into mine because you'll find out I cheated on my diet today, and yesterday, and the day before that. I'm definitely flunking Diet 101, but I wouldn't care to advertise that fact."

"Got it," Carolyn said, sitting down in the chair behind the desk. "I'll take your mind off my list of those I intend to peer into."

"You're cuckoo," Janice said, then left the office.

"I know," Carolyn said, sighing. "A certain

Mr. Sharpe has tipped me over the edge of my sanity.''

She took the first packet of papers from the stack, set it in front of her, then stared into space.

If she really could read minds, she thought, she'd delve into Ryan's. She'd discover his innermost secrets, what had happened to him to cause him such deep pain about his heritage, about being different.

"Erase that," she said, shaking her head.

Even if she had that mystical power, she wouldn't use it. No, Ryan's secrets were his to keep. But, oh, dear heaven, she wished he trusted and believed in her enough to share them. And taking that one step further, she wished she had the courage to tell him about her hearing aids.

Enough of this, she thought, directing her attention to the papers in front of her. She had work to do. There were six baby girls on the other side of the world waiting to become part of a loving family. Six baby girls waiting to come home.

The image of standing with Ryan on the hill where he intended to build his house suddenly took front row center in Carolyn's mind.

Home, she thought. Waiting to come home.

Carolyn frowned in self-disgust.

The house that Ryan was designing had nothing to do with her. Nothing at all.

Chapter Six

Saturday's weather was absolutely perfect for an outdoor activity.

Ryan parked on the street in front of his grandparents' home at the end of a long line of cars, then assisted Carolyn from the vehicle. They made their way up the long drive as Carolyn remarked on the gorgeous, sloping lawn.

She was doing fine, she told herself. Ryan didn't have a clue that she was entertaining a convention of butterflies in her stomach over meeting his enormous family.

"Don't even try to remember everyone's name

today," Ryan said, as he opened the gate leading to the backyard. "No one can do that on the first go, but after you attend a few of these get-togethers you'll be putting names with faces like a pro."

Carolyn looked up at Ryan quickly, wondering if he realized what his words implied.

Before she could dwell on his statement further, they were greeted by shouts and waves. Ryan encircled Carolyn's shoulders and led her around the yard, introducing her to so many people—from grandparents to babies—that it all became a blur. She smiled, nodded, said it was a pleasure, then finally sank gratefully onto a lawn chair.

"Would you like some soda?" Ryan said.

"Yes, thank you," she said, smiling up at him. "That sounds good."

"Save that chair next to you for me. Threaten bodily harm to anyone who tries to snatch it before I get back."

"Oh, okay." Carolyn laughed.

Ryan hadn't taken more than two steps when an attractive blond woman slid onto the chair in question. Ryan caught the motion out of the corner of his eye and spun back around, planting his hands on his hips.

"That's my chair, Jessica," he said, attempting and failing to appear extremely stern. "Out."

"Shoo, shoo," Jessica said, flapping her hands

at him. "Go do whatever you were going to do while I tell Carolyn about what a rotten little kid you were, cousin."

"Don't believe a word she says, Carolyn. She's an attorney and you know what kind of reputation they have. They bend the truth to suit their fancy."

"Daniel," Jessica yelled. "Arrest Ryan for slander, the rotten so-and-so."

"Can't," Daniel called from across the yard. "I'm a homicide detective, sweetheart. I'm useless unless you've got a dead body to tell me about."

"That can be arranged," Jessica said, glaring at Ryan.

Ryan hooted with laughter and continued on his way.

"Do you think you'll survive us?" Jessica said, smiling at Carolyn. "Ryan has never brought a date to any of our gatherings before, and we're all so delighted that you're here."

"Thank you," Carolyn said, then paused. "Ryan has never brought a date to… Really?"

"Really," Jessica said, nodding. "So. Fill me in. How did you meet cousin Ryan? Oh, and when? How long have you two been going out with each other? Let's see. What else do I need to know?"

Carolyn laughed. "Yep, you're definitely an attorney." She narrowed her eyes. "Jessica. Jessica

MacAllister Quinn, married to Daniel, mother of Tessa, the cute toddler over there by her daddy.''

"And another Quinn on the way," Jessica said, patting her flat stomach. "Very good, Carolyn. I know it's difficult to keep us all straight at first. We're a very big family."

"And a very nice family," Carolyn said. "Everyone has made me feel so welcome. I was admittedly nervous about coming here today, but I'm already comfortable and having a great time."

"Super," Jessica said. "Now, start at the top. How did you meet Ryan?"

Across the yard Ryan retrieved two cans of soda from a metal tub. He felt a hand clamp onto his shoulder and turned to see his father.

"Hi, Dad," Ryan said, smiling. "How are you? And how's Mom?"

"We're doing fine, considering our advancing years," Ted Sharpe said. "Carolyn St. John is a very pretty young woman, son. It's nice to see you with someone at one of these functions. Anything I should know about you and the lovely Ms. St. John?"

"Once a cop, always a cop," Ryan said, laughing as he shook the cold water from the cans of soda he was holding. "But I guess I'm not surprised that I'm creating a buzz by bringing Carolyn here today. She's just… Well, the first woman I've ever dated who I felt would fit in with the family, have a good time. All the other women were sort of…''

"Snooty?" Ted said, raising his eyebrows.

Ryan laughed. "Something like that. Carolyn is down-to-earth, real, like the rest of us, if you know what I mean. She's a very special lady."

"Mmm," Ted said, nodding. "Sounds a tad serious, if I dare offer that opinion."

"Oh, now don't get nuts, Dad. Carolyn and I are dating, enjoying each other's company, end of story. I'm not interested in a serious relationship with anyone." He glanced around the large yard. "I see Mom over there, but where's my sister? She'll be in line to give me the third degree about Carolyn, that's for sure."

"Patty said she'd come if she could, but she wasn't certain she could make it."

"Again?" Ryan said, meeting his father's troubled gaze. "That was the pat answer she gave all through the holidays, and more often than not she didn't show up."

"I know. Your mother and I are quite concerned about it. We're afraid that perhaps Patty and Peter might be having some marital problems. I don't know what to think, Ryan. Whenever we ask her how she is, Patty just smiles and says everything is fine. She does, however, seem to be keeping a distance between herself and the rest of the family."

"Maybe I'll drop by and see her one of these days...soon."

Ted nodded. "That's a good idea. You two have always been very close, and perhaps she'll tell you what's going on. If there is a problem there, it might be easier to confide in her brother than to feel like she's running to Mommy and Daddy."

Ryan nodded. "I'll make it a point to connect with her, Dad, but if Patty tells me something, then makes me promise to keep it to myself, then..." He shrugged.

"I realize that. I'm hoping you'll be able to re-assure your decrepit parents that their baby girl is all right."

Ryan laughed. "Would you knock it off with this bit about you and mom being old? Sixty isn't exactly over the hill." He paused and his expression became serious. "Dad, I wonder if I could speak with you privately in the house for a few minutes?"

"Well, sure, of course."

Ryan looked across the yard, then placed the soda cans back into the tub.

"Carolyn looks relaxed, at ease, despite the fact Jessica is no doubt giving her a thorough cross-examination. I don't think Carolyn will mind if I disappear for a bit.''

"Let's go into your grandfather's study. There have been a multitude of private conversations in that special room over the years.''

In what was considered Robert MacAllister's special place, Ted sank onto one of a pair of matching chairs flanking a fireplace. He watched as Ryan wandered around the room, touching a lamp, peering at books on the shelves, running his hand over the soft leather of the top of the chair opposite where his father sat.

"You're stalling,'' Ted said.

"Yep,'' Ryan said, then sank onto the chair. He rested his elbows on his knees, clasped his hands, then stared into the empty hearth for several long moments before meeting his father's gaze. "I need you ask you something.''

"Okay.''

"We've all heard the great story, many, many times about how you delivered Patty before the paramedics could arrive. It's a very special tale, and I've already shared it with Carolyn because it's special, should be retold.''

Ted smiled. "It was definitely one of the highlights of my life.''

"With just cause,'' Ryan said, nodding. "Awesome. Even though you aren't Patty's biological father, the minute you saw her you said something like 'You're my daughter. You're mine.' That makes sense, you know, because you were with Mom during the last stages of her pregnancy and then you witnessed Patty taking her first breath and…the bond was instantaneous. You considered her your child."

"Yes, I did."

"Which brings me to my question, Dad. It took months of paperwork before you could go to Korea and adopt me. You didn't witness my first breath or my first smile or my first tooth. I was six months old when you saw me, held me. I had a personality of sorts, I suppose, likes, dislikes, a bunch a stuff you didn't have a clue about. You didn't know who I was."

Ted frowned, but didn't speak.

"What I want, need, to know is how long did it take before you bonded with me? Really felt like I was your son? I need a honest answer, Dad, not what you think I should hear. Was it months? Even years?"

Ted leaned forward. "You don't know the answer to that question? You're asking me this because you honestly don't know? I've never told you? Oh, God, Ryan, I'm sorry. I can't believe we didn't talk about this when you were a little boy.

"I guess I knew in my heart and head what the truth was and somewhere along the line assumed I'd told you, the same way I told Patty about her birth and... Damn it, saying I'm sorry doesn't cut it."

"Dad, just answer the question, would you? It's important to me."

"Of course, it is. Yes." Ted sank back in the chair. "Ryan, picture if you can my heart being like a puzzle with one piece missing. Can you do that?"

"Yeah, okay."

"In the orphanage in Korea, your mother and I were in a small, sparsely furnished room, that needed a coat of paint. It seemed like an eternity from the time the head of the place told us to wait in that room and the door finally opened again.

"And suddenly there you were," Ted said, his voice husky with emotion. "The woman carried you in, and you were frowning, looked mad as hell, stared at me and stuck your thumb in your mouth.

"I looked at you, Ryan, and the piece that had been missing from my heart clicked into place because at that very moment I became complete. I had a son. You. I took you in my arms, you stiffened up and I whispered 'Don't be afraid, Ryan. Daddy is here. Daddy is here, son.' And you laid your head on my shoulder. I'll never forget that moment. Never. It's as meaningful to me, as important and special, as helping Patty come into the world."

"I..." Ryan said, then shook his head and stopped speaking as an achy sensation closed his throat.

"My son," Ted whispered, tears filling his eyes as he relived precious memories. "Then, now, always."

"I didn't know," Ryan said, his voice raspy. "It's just like the Fosters and Elizabeth, but I thought that was a fluke. I figured it took you and Mom a long time to bond with me because you didn't get me as a newborn baby, and on top of that I was...I was different and—"

"The only difference between you and Patty," Ted said, "is that you were my son and she was my daughter. You were a boy, she was a girl. That's it."

Ryan nodded slowly, then turned his head away from his father's view as he realized that two tears had fallen onto his cheeks.

Ted got to his feet. "I love you so much, Ryan. I'm more sorry than I can ever begin to tell you that we didn't have this discussion years and years ago. Forgive me. Please."

Ryan swiped his hands over his face and rose to

step into his father's embrace. They hugged—man and man, father and son.

"I love you, too, Dad," Ryan whispered. "Thank you for sharing all this with me. I...well, thank you."

They stepped apart, nodded, and made no attempt to hide fresh tears that filled their eyes.

"Well," Ryan said, then cleared his throat. "I'd best go rescue Carolyn before she thinks I deserted her. I'll let you know if I find out anything I can tell you from Patty. See ya."

Ryan left the room and Ted drew a shuddering breath.

"See ya," he said, "my son."

When he was certain he had his emotions under control, Ted returned to the backyard, found Hannah and pulled her close to his side.

"What's the matter, honey?" she said, searching Ted's face.

"Nothing," Ted said. "A wrong has been set to rights, that's all."

Ryan retrieved the cans of soda from the tub and made his way across the yard toward Carolyn. He took a deep breath and let it out slowly as he went, reliving the conversation he'd just had. He knew he'd go over and over it many times again in his mind in the days to come.

When Jessica saw Ryan striding toward her with a very determined expression on his face, she got to her feet and made a big production of dusting off the lawn chair.

"Ta-ta," she said, waggling her fingers at Ryan before he got too close. "I have a daughter who needs a dry diaper. Catch you later, cousin."

Ryan snagged two paper cups as he went by a table, then finally sank onto the lawn chair next to Carolyn, handing her a can and cup.

"I'm sorry I was gone so long, Carolyn. How bad was it? Did Jessica whip out a bare lightbulb and dangle it over your head?"

"Close, very close." Carolyn laughed. "Jessica must be awesome in court."

"She's good, no doubt about it. She and her partner, Mary-Clair, specialize in representing women with legal problems. You know, spousal abuse, custody issues, not getting child support, that sort of thing. They're gaining a reputation for being very tough, very savvy and very dedicated.

"Mary-Clair is married to Connor O'Shea now. But she was Mary-Clair Cavelli before, and that huge family is considered part of our clan, too. I don't see any of them here today, though. They must have had something else on their calendars."

"Thank goodness. I won't remember even half

of the names of the people I met, let alone add another whole bunch.''

"Are you enjoying yourself?'' Ryan said, looking at her intently.

"Oh, yes, Ryan, I am,'' she said, smiling at him warmly. "There is so much love, so much caring here you can almost reach out and touch it like it was a living entity. You're so fortunate to have grown up in the midst of this wonderful family.''

"Yeah,'' Ryan said, looking off into the distance. "I realize that, believe me I do.'' He paused, then looked at her again. "Carolyn, there's something I want to say to you. I'm an architect. I draw up plans so that houses can be built for people. But you? You help create families that turn those houses into homes filled with love and laughter. I understand now why you're so dedicated to your career, your life's work, and I want you to know that I truly respect what you do.''

"Thank you, Ryan,'' Carolyn said, struggling against threatening tears. "That means so much to me to hear you say that.''

"Yeah. Hey, no more heavy stuff today,'' he said, smiling. "We're here to enjoy ourselves and eat too much. Wait until you taste my grandfather's hamburgers. You're in for a real treat, my sweet. He has a secret recipe he shares with no one.''

Secrets, Carolyn thought, pouring some soda

into her cup. Always there was what Ryan wasn't telling her about what had made him stand apart from this marvelous, loving family.

Oh, Ryan, what is it? What happened?

No, she thought in the next instant. He was right. No heavy stuff today. She was simply going to enjoy being here with Ryan's family.

Enjoy every moment spent with him.

Chapter Seven

As the party progressed, Carolyn began to feel as though she'd known Ryan's family for a very long time.

The hamburgers that Robert MacAllister cooked on the grill in the corner of the yard were indeed delicious. There were also big bowls of chips, relishes, several choices of salad and an enormous four-layer chocolate cake with swirling white frosting for dessert.

Carolyn helped clear the long table and carry the remaining food—although there was little of that— into the house, chatting comfortably with the others as they completed the chores.

The men and the older children began games of Frisbee and horseshoes, but Carolyn and the other women sank onto lawn chairs set close together.

"Oh, I'm so full," Carolyn said. "I won't need to eat for a week. Everything was delicious, and I definitely made a piggy of myself."

"We're delighted that you enjoyed the meal," Margaret MacAllister said. "My husband, the hamburger chef, is hinting that he might leave the recipe for his burgers to one of the family in his will. I said something wifely like 'that's nice, dear,' while thinking it was silliest thing I've ever heard."

"It is not," Robert MacAllister said, coming up behind her. He settled onto a lawn chair. "I might bequeath the recipe to the Smithsonian. I haven't made up my mind yet about that." He paused. "I'm joining your hen party, ladies, because preparing that culinary masterpiece wore me out and I'm not up to Frisbee or horseshoes."

"Another humble cook," Carolyn said, laughing. "Just like Ryan is."

"Oh?" Emily MacAllister Maxwell said. "Ryan has prepared a meal for you, Carolyn?"

"Well, I...well, yes," Carolyn said, feeling a warm flush creep onto her cheeks. "Omelet. He made a fantastic omelet after we bought fresh produce at a farmers' market, and…I think I'm sorry I opened my mouth.''

Margaret laughed. "Leave poor Carolyn alone. We're all glad she's here, it's nice to see Ryan smiling so much, and that is that.''

"But, Grandma,'' Emily said, "we want to know—''

"Em…i…ly,'' Margaret said sternly.

"Okay,'' Emily said, sinking back in her chair. "Oh, hey, did you see that Frisbee catch Trevor just made? Maybe they'll enter Frisbee games in the Olympics and he'll win a gold metal. My son the Olympic champ. How's that?''

"The way he's coming along with his swimming with Mark coaching him,'' Robert said, "he may enter the Olympics at some point in the future as a fish.'' He paused. "No, I don't think having that kind of pressure is good for a young person. Well, time will tell what he'll do with his natural abilities.''

As the group shifted their attention to the games in progress, one of the younger children ran by the group of chairs and blew hard on a silver whistle attached to a cord around his neck.

The shrill sound caused Carolyn's hearing aids to shriek painfully, and her hands flew up to cover her ears. She looked over to see that both Margaret and Robert had done exactly the same thing.

When Carolyn's gaze met Margaret's, Carolyn dropped her hands back into her lap and averted her eyes from Margaret's. Carolyn glanced at the others and was relieved to see that no one else had seen what had taken place.

An hour later the games ended with the announcement from the participants that they were ready for more soda and cake.

Margaret got to her feet. "Why don't you help me bring out the dessert, Carolyn? I think there's enough of that cake left to go around one more time. If not I made a big batch of sugar cookies to fill tummies."

Carolyn followed Margaret into the kitchen, where Margaret turned to smile gently at Carolyn.

"You're wearing hearing aids, aren't you, dear? That whistle certainly set off a painful screech, didn't it? Robert and I have had our hearing aids for several years and know what excessive noise can do. Have you worn yours for long?"

"Yes. Since I was a little girl."

"I see." Margaret reached for a stack of paper plates.

"Ryan doesn't know that I'm hearing impaired."

Margaret left the plates on the counter and turned to look at Carolyn with a frown.

"Why on earth not? It's certainly nothing to be

ashamed of. Why haven't you told Ryan that you wear hearing aids?''

"Because if I did," Carolyn said, her voice trembling slightly, "what Ryan and I are sharing would be over.''

"I don't understand, dear," Margaret said, shaking her head.

"Margaret, Ryan is struggling to accept his heritage, the fact that he is different. He'll want nothing to do with me once he knows that *I'm* different in such a severe manner.''

"Oh, my darling child," Margaret said, taking Carolyn's hands in her own. "I simply can't believe that is true.''

"It *is* true.''

"But secrets kept have the power to destroy, Carolyn," Margaret said, tightening her hold on Carolyn's hands.

"I know that, Margaret, but Ryan has his own secrets, too. He's never confided in me, told me what happened to cause him to have such problems, suffer such pain about his heritage.

"So we're both concealing something we're not willing to share with each other. But it's all right because...because what Ryan and I have is temporary. I have no delusions about a permanent future with him. None. Once he knows about my hearing problem, that will be that. I'm just not prepared to say goodbye to him yet because... I'm just not.''

''But you two care deeply for each other,'' Margaret said, giving Carolyn's hands a little shake. ''That's apparent to all of us by the way you smile at each other, the tender looks you exchange, the natural way you stand so close together because it's where you know you belong.

''Oh, Carolyn, you and Ryan both need to listen to your hearts. You need to pay attention to your feelings *and* the whispers that will tell you that those secrets you're each keeping are dangerous, threatening the very foundation of what you and Ryan are building together in your relationship.''

''We don't *have* a relationship in the sense you're referring to, Margaret,'' Carolyn said, her voice rising. ''Please, listen to me. Ryan and I are together temporarily and...I don't mean to be rude, but I really don't wish to discuss this further.''

''All right, dear.'' Margaret released Carolyn's hands. ''It's time for me to mind my own business. But would you at least think about what I said? Realize that secrets kept can destroy...''

''No,'' Carolyn interrupted. ''Secrets kept can't destroy something that isn't there.'' She paused. ''Let's get this dessert outside, shall we? Everyone will be wondering what we're doing in here.''

Margaret sighed. ''Despite the popular belief

these days, problems can't be solved by consuming great quantities of chocolate.''

''But it can certainly take a person's mind off their woes,'' Carolyn said, producing a small smile. ''Thank you for caring so much, Margaret, but you're worrying about something that doesn't even apply to Ryan and me.''

''Mmm,'' Margaret said, frowning as she picked up the paper plates again and handed a platter of sugar cookies to Carolyn.

When Carolyn and Margaret returned to the yard with the eagerly awaited treat, they discovered that another MacAllister had arrived.

''Well, Matt,'' Margaret said, smiling. ''Isn't this a nice surprise? You're just in time for another go-round of calories. Oh, and this is Carolyn St. John. She's Ryan's...she came with Ryan today.''

''Hello,'' Carolyn said, smiling as she set the platter of sugar cookies on the table. ''It's a pleasure to meet you, Matt.''

Another handsome MacAllister, she thought. This family was certainly made up of extremely attractive people. Matt MacAllister was tall, well built, had rugged features, compelling brown eyes and dark-auburn hair.

''The feeling is mutual,'' Matt said, smiling.

"Whoa. Look at those desserts. I sure have great timing, even though I missed Grandpa's hamburgers."

"Hi, sweet guy," a woman said, coming to Matt's side and standing on tiptoe to kiss him on the cheek. "How's my twin brother today? And why are you dressed in a suit and tie for a backyard barbecue?"

"Hi, nosy Noel," Matt said, sinking onto a lawn chair after grabbing a handful of cookies. "To answer your questions, I'm fine. As for the yuppie attire, as the public relations director extraordinaire of Mercy Hospital, I've been at a news conference regarding case number 1419."

"You're doing it again," Noel said, with a cluck of disgust. "You're talking in terms of case numbers like a CIA agent or something."

"Oh, sorry," Matt said. "It's just habit, I guess. Every situation I deal with, good, bad and in between is assigned a case number, and that's how I view them in my mind, keep them all straight. It's no big deal."

"Yes, it is," Noel said, "because those numbers represent living, breathing people and—"

"Don't squabble, you two," Margaret said. "Matt, eat a cookie."

"Yes, ma'am," Matt said, and popped a cookie into his mouth.

"Okay," Noel said, with a dramatic sigh, "we'll

do this your way, Matt…this time. Do tell, dear brother, what case number whatever is all about.''

"It's a very nice case number," Matt said. "A little boy who will be arriving from Korea is going to have heart surgery at the hospital, all expenses paid.

"We did the press bit today, complete with film at eleven, with the director of Hands across the Sea International Adoptions who worked with me to organize this pro bono project. The director, Elizabeth Kane, is leaving tomorrow for the Philippines to attend a conference on international adoptions, and the boy doesn't get here until Monday.

"So!" Matt went on. "We did the press thing today, plus we didn't want the child to be overwhelmed by a bunch of people when he arrives. Hence, the suit and tie. I saw a picture of the kid. He's really a cute little boy. His name is…"

"Kimiko Sung," Carolyn said, then felt a rush of embarrassed heat flush her cheeks. "Oh, I'm sorry. I didn't mean to interrupt you, Matt. Kimiko's name just popped out of my mouth. I work at Hands across the Sea."

"No joke?" Matt said, raising his eyebrows. "Well, small world, huh?"

The remainder of the family had gathered by the table to have more dessert and were listening intently to the discussion about Kimiko Sung.

"You didn't mention anything about this little boy," Ryan said to Carolyn, as everyone sat down.

"I'm not closely involved in the situation. Elizabeth coordinated it all. She learned about Kimiko, the fact that he needed heart surgery and his parents are unable to afford it, and took it from there. There's a host family who will pick up Kimiko at the airport, and he'll stay with them before and after the surgery until he's able to go home to Korea."

Matt nodded. "The host family was at the press conference today. Nice people. They have a teenage son and a daughter about ten years old. The surgeon is donating his time, all hospital costs will be covered by us and another organization is picking up the tab for Kimiko's plane fare. It's good public relations for everyone, plus a little boy gets a much-needed operation."

"How old is this child?" Margaret said. "And what exactly is wrong with his heart?"

"He's five," Matt said, "but he's small for his age. He has a heart defect call ventricular septal, which in layman's terms means a hole in his heart. Sometimes they close on their own, and that's the happy ending of the story. In Kimiko's case, the hole didn't close and must be corrected surgically."

"Oh, that poor baby," Margaret said. "Just

imagine how frightened he will be when he arrives. He's separated from his parents, he'll undergo an operation, won't be able to understand one comforting word that might be said to him. I'm delighted to hear that his problem is going to be corrected, but I do worry about how terrifying it will be.''

"Elizabeth thought of that,'' Carolyn said. "The host family has been studying the Korean language so they can communicate with Kimiko. Hopefully that will ease his fears a bit. They have a room set up for him at their home with lots of toys. Their attention will be centered on him while he's here, and he'll get oodles of love and hugs. Lots and lots of hugs.''

"There you go,'' Matt said, smiling. "You must have kids of your own, Carolyn. You know how important those hugs are to those short folks.''

"No. I'm not a mother, but I do know what a hug can do for both the short *and* tall in this world.''

"Amen to that,'' Ryan said, nodding. "Well, I hope everything goes as it should for Kimiko Sung. He's a lucky little guy.''

"Hear, hear,'' Robert said, raising his paper cup. "Let's make a toast to Kimiko and everyone who is involved in making it possible for that child to lead a happy, normal life.''

The toast was made by all, then chatter erupted as they spoke among themselves about the heart-tugging situation regarding Kimiko.

No, Carolyn thought dismally, I don't have children, will never be a mother. I would be a good mother, devoted and loving, I know I would, but I've learned the bitter truth already that a man won't believe that someone with my handicap could take proper care of his child. I'll be left with empty arms and an aching heart for a baby I'll never have.

"Carolyn? Is something wrong? You look rather upset."

"Oh, no, I'm fine, Ryan. I was just thinking about Kimiko, plus the fact that it's quite a coincidence that a member of your family is involved in the whole thing."

Ryan laughed. "That comes from our being a very large family. You bump into us all over the place."

"And you come in pairs and threesomes. Jessica, Emily and Alice are triplets, and Matt just said that Noel is his twin. Gracious."

"There are two sets of twins in that family," Ryan said, smiling. "Jeff and Kate are a dynamic duo who are five years younger than Matt and Noel. Their parents, Andrea and John, are away on vacation right now."

"They go on vacation a lot," Matt said. "They're still resting up from raising the four of us." He paused and pulled off his tie, stuffing it in the pocket of his jacket. "Man, I'm beat. If I nod off, just cover me with a blanket and wake me in the morning. Vacation. That word is music to my ears, but it's sure not on my calendar in the near future."

"You work too hard, Matt," Noel said. "You have an extremely high-stress career and you never take a break, and you're going to pay the piper if you don't—"

"Halt," Matt said, raising both hands to silence his sister. "Having Mom and Dad away on a trip means I don't have to listen to that lecture. You aren't allowed to pick up that ball while they're away."

"Well!" Noel said indignantly. "You don't have to get grumpy about it."

"Yes, I do," he said, tugging on a strand of her hair. "It's the only way to get you to put a cork in it." He shifted his gaze to Carolyn. "You sure are pretty, Ms. St. John. What are you doing hanging out with a dud like my cousin Ryan?"

"Here we go," Ryan said, rolling his eyes. "Stuff a cookie in your mouth, Matt."

Matt chuckled and did as instructed, following that cookie with another one.

"You and Matt are very close friends, aren't you?" Carolyn said softly to Ryan.

"Yeah. He's a good man. Noel is right, though, he works much too hard. I'd bet a buck those cookies are the first food he's bothered to eat today. Whatever Matt does, he does to the max." He laughed. "Including giving me a hard time whenever the opportunity presents itself."

"Great cookies, Grandma," Matt said, reaching for a can of soda. "I just took care of breakfast, lunch and dinner with your superb sugar cookies."

"I rest my case," Ryan said to Carolyn.

"Hey, Ryan," Matt said, "I hear you're finally drawing up the plans to build your dream house on that land you own. This is the big year, huh? Listen, you gotta make room for a pool table when you're doing your thing with your trusty pencil. Don't forget. Pool table."

"Oh, phooey on that," Jessica said. "He should have a hot tub on an outside deck. Talk about romantic. Sit in the swirling water, sip champagne, stare up at the stars with a special someone. Oh, yes, a hot tub."

"No, no," Noel said. "Ryan should concentrate on the kitchen. He's a super cook and should have state-of-the-art everything in an enormous kitchen, then invite me to dinner...a lot."

Carolyn laughed in delight as everyone began to

add their two cents regarding Ryan's house. He sat beside her smiling and shaking his head.

A warmth swept through her as she replayed in her mind what Ryan had said about her career making it possible for houses to be transformed into homes with a family, with love and laughter.

And there was so much love and caring in *this* family, she thought. It just seemed impossible that Ryan's heritage could have been a stumbling block for him given the love emanating from these marvelous people.

But then again, being different was extremely powerful—unbelievably so at times.

And being different could be so very, very lonely.

The remainder of the afternoon was made up of ongoing conversation about a multitude of subjects, more Frisbee competition and polishing off every crumb of the cake and cookies.

The temperature began to drop as a gorgeous sunset began to streak across the sky. Everyone pitched in to put the backyard in order and clean the kitchen.

With choruses of farewells, accompanied by hugs and promises to get together again soon, a mass exodus was made through the gate, and vehicles were driven away like a parade. Ryan beeped the horn as a final goodbye as he pulled out of the line and headed in the direction of Carolyn's apartment.

"I had such a nice time today," Carolyn said. "Thank you for inviting me to go with you."

"You're welcome, and I'm glad you enjoyed yourself. You sure made a hit with my family, too." He paused. "What would you like to do about dinner? We could stop and pick up a pizza or Chinese food or whatever strikes your fancy."

"I couldn't eat a thing." Carolyn patted her stomach. "I'm stuffed full of your grandmother's delicious sugar cookies. Are *you* hungry?"

"Not at the moment," Ryan said, laughing. "I had cookies *and* another slice of that cake."

"I was going to be very polite and not mention that fact."

"Well, I can't delay ending this outing by our having dinner," Ryan said, glancing over at Carolyn, "so I'll just jump in and say that I'd like to spend the evening with you. Play cards? Watch a movie on television? The ball, Ms. St. John, is now in your court as far as deciding if I bid you adieu in about ten minutes, or hang around awhile."

"I'd like you to stay. I'm sure we'll think of something to do."

Oh, good grief, she thought in the next instant, talk about a double entendre. Maybe Ryan hadn't picked up on how risqué that had sounded.

"Now *that* was a very loaded statement, ma'am," Ryan said, chuckling.

So much for that wish, Carolyn thought. Ryan had *definitely* picked up on how risqué that had sounded. The really wanton part of this whole back-and-forth blither was that in all honesty she'd said exactly what she'd meant to.

She wanted Ryan to stay. She wanted to make love with Ryan Sharpe. There was actually no double entendre about it. Her desire for Ryan was earthy, real and honest. But how in the world did she get that information across to him? Tearing off her clothes would be a big clue, but she wasn't that brave, not even close.

Oh, great, she mentally rambled on, the butterfly convention was back in full force. Her lack of experience and sophistication was just so...so annoying.

Neither Carolyn nor Ryan spoke as he parked in the lot at her apartment building, went through the front door, rode up in the elevator, walked down the hall and entered her apartment.

Carolyn stood to one side as Ryan followed her in, then stepped forward to shut the door. As she turned to look at him, she gasped in surprise as he closed the distance between them, causing her to thud against the door. He braced one hand on either side of her head and looked directly into her eyes that had widened with surprise at the abrupt motion.

"Can't do it," he said, his voice slightly gritty. "I can't handle spending the next hours sitting close to you on the sofa watching a movie, nor can I concentrate on playing gin rummy or whatever."

"I…"

"Just listen a minute, okay?" he said, his body only inches from Carolyn.

"'Kay," she said, her heart beginning to beat in a wild tempo due to Ryan's close proximity.

"I want you, Carolyn St. John," he said. "I desire you more than I have any woman before. Kissing you good-night at this door and walking away has turned into torture in its purest form.

"Then when I get home I can't sleep, just toss and turn, aching for you. I want to make love with you more than I can even begin to describe. I think I'd better just leave. Now. Right now. Because if I stay…" His voice trailed off and he shook his head.

"No," Carolyn whispered.

"Clear enough," Ryan said, dropping his hands to his sides and taking a step back. "I'll shove off. I really enjoyed being with you today and I want you to know that, believe that. I'll talk to you soon and—"

"No."

"Ah, man, you don't even want to hear from me because I said I wanted to make love with you?"

"Ryan, you're misunderstanding me." Carolyn took a step forward and framed his face with hands that were not quite steady. She drew a shuddering breath and lifted her chin. "The *no* was *no* I don't want you to go. And *no* I don't want to play cards or watch a movie.

"I've never done anything so brazen before in my life, but...here I go. Ryan, I want you, too. I desire you beyond measure, want to make love with you, can't bear the thought of another seemingly endless night wishing that you were next to me and...

"Oh, damn, damn, I can feel the heat on my cheeks," Carolyn said miserably, dropping her hands from his face. "I'm blushing like an adolescent, despite the womanly things I'm saying. I'm about as worldly and sophisticated as a rock. I'm mortified, so embarrassed because I'm not doing this well at all."

Carolyn sighed. "Do I get any points for being honest at least? I do want you, Ryan, want to make love with you. I do. And I think I'm running out of oxygen because I'm talking so much, and there is a whole bunch of butterflies who keep showing up in my stomach and doing the two-step and—"

Ryan kissed her.

He cut off her high-speed dissertation by pulling her into his arms, nestling her to his body, and covering her lips with his in a searing kiss.

Oh, thank goodness, Carolyn thought, encircling his neck with her hands, sinking her fingers into his thick hair and returning the kiss in total abandon. Ryan was not—was most definitely not—rejecting her. He wanted her just as much as she desired him.

They were going to make love together, glorious, wondrous, equally-agreed-upon love. She refused to think. She was just going to feel. Savor. Tuck the memories of this night away in a safe place in her heart.

Ryan broke the kiss and took a ragged breath. "Are you sure? Will you, can you, promise me you'll have no regrets about this? I couldn't handle it if you were sorry later, Carolyn. You have to be certain that—"

"Now you're the one who is going to run out of oxygen," she said, smiling at him warmly. "I promise you, Ryan, that I'll have no regrets. I promise you that I am very, very sure that this is right and good and meant to be. I want to make love with you, Ryan Sharpe. Now. Right now."

Chapter Eight

Something magical seemed to happen as Carolyn and Ryan crossed the living room and started down the hallway to the bedroom with his arm encircling her shoulders to keep her tucked close to his side.

With each step they took the world beyond the two of them disappeared in a hazy, sensual mist that swirled around them, encasing them in a warm and gentle cocoon.

With each step they took, the sense of rightness, of being where they belonged together, heightened, as did the desire thrumming within them.

With each step, they stilled the niggling voices

in their minds so that their doubts wouldn't gain entrance into the private world created just for them.

Carolyn's bedroom was a feminine delight of pastel wildflowers on the bedspread and the double bed's matching skirt that fell to the floor in soft folds. There was a round table beside a white wicker rocking chair with a puffy pillow on the seat. A small lamp with a shade made of stained glass echoing the tones of the flowers graced the oak nightstand.

Carolyn stepped free of Ryan's embrace to snap on the lamp, casting a golden glow over the room. She turned to look at him, not quite meeting his gaze.

"This room is rather—girly, I guess," she said, her voice trembling slightly. "I decorated it just the way I wanted it, and I hope it doesn't make you feel uncomfortable. Or as though you don't belong in such a frilly place or… Oh, dear."

"Hey," Ryan said, closing the distance between them and framing Carolyn's face in his hands. "You're nervous, aren't you?" He smiled. "Well, guess what? So am I. I want this to be perfect for you, me, us. This room is lovely. This room is you." He paused. "Carolyn, if you've changed your mind about—"

"No, oh, no," she said, looking directly into his

eyes. "I'm just nervous, like you said. I don't have a great deal of experience regarding... What I mean is, I told you that I'm not a worldly, sophisticated woman or anything like that and...oh, Ryan, just kiss me so I'll quit blithering like an idiot."

"Yes, ma'am," he said, then lowered his head and captured her lips with his.

The swirling, misty magic increased its power, whisking away Carolyn's self-doubts along with the remaining butterflies.

Ryan broke the kiss and swept back the spread and blanket, revealing pale yellow sheets that represented the sun, to nurture the flowers.

As though standing outside of herself, Carolyn watched as their clothes seemed to float from their bodies.

They stood before each other naked, gazes sweeping over the other, breaths catching and hearts racing as they etched indelibly in their minds all that they saw, all that would be theirs.

"You're beautiful, Carolyn St. John," Ryan said, his voice gritty.

"You're magnificent, Ryan Sharpe," she whispered.

Ryan lifted her into his arms, kissed her deeply, then laid her in the center of the bed, following her down and catching his weight on one forearm as he stretched out next to her. He reached back to the floor to retrieve a foil packet from his wallet, then returned to cover Carolyn's body with his, keeping his weight braced on his bent arms.

"There's something magical about this night," he said. "Something I've never felt before, nor can I explain what it is, but it's here, with us." He frowned. "That must sound crazy."

"No, it doesn't," Carolyn said, wrapping her arms around his neck. "I feel it, too. It's...ours."

Ryan's mouth melted over Carolyn's, and all further thought fled, leaving only the want, the need, the desire that burned and churned and licked within them with hot, enticing flames.

He shifted lower to lave the nipple of one of Carolyn's breasts with his tongue, and she closed her eyes to savor every exquisite sensation coursing throughout her. He paid homage to her other breast, then trailed a ribbon of kisses down the flat plane of her stomach, causing her to shiver in anticipation of all that was yet to come.

They touched. Explored. Gloried in the discoveries made. Left heated paths with caressing fingertips that were followed by lips that fanned the fire.

Ryan's muscles quivered from forced restraint, his focus on Carolyn, on his fierce determination that her pleasure must come first before he sought the release his body ached for.

Carolyn tossed her head restlessly on the pillow, a near sob catching in her throat as passion consumed her to the point she could hardly breathe.

She was acutely aware of the softness of her own body and the taut rugged strength of Ryan's, marveling at the differences that somehow made them a perfect match.

She inhaled Ryan's aroma of soap and fresh air, and something undefinable that was uniquely him and masculine beyond measure.

She flicked her tongue over his skin, tasting the tangy salt from the moist sheen.

She heard the groan that rumbled deep in his chest, and her name escape from his lips like a prayer.

Never, she thought, had she felt so vibrantly alive, so grateful to be a woman, so as to be a counterpart to this magnificent man.

Ryan.

"Please," she said, a sob catching in her throat. "Please, Ryan."

He nodded, unable to speak, then left her only long enough to ensure that he protected her, then moved over and into her with a powerful thrust that filled her. He began to move, slowly at first, then increasing the tempo.

Harder. Faster. Reaching for the summit where more wildflowers awaited to receive them.

Carolyn clung to Ryan's shoulders as she matched the wild rhythm, beat for beat, feeling herself soaring closer to a place she had never been before, but knowing it was where she had to be...with Ryan.

Carolyn, Ryan's mind hummed. Carolyn. Nothing he had ever known compared to what he was experiencing. Nothing had held this intensity, this feeling of completeness, of emotions intertwined with the physical ecstasy, making it impossible to separate one from the other. It was magic. It was Carolyn.

They burst upon the bed of wildflowers seconds apart, calling the name of the other, feeling the soft petals float across their bodies and the warming sun cascade over them. It was a place of splendor that belonged only to them.

Magic.

They hovered, drifted, swayed in a delicate breeze that cooled them and carried them gently back.

Ryan collapsed against Carolyn, spent, sated, then gathered his last ounce of strength to roll off her, tucking her close to his side, her head nestled on his shoulder. He fumbled for the sheet and blanket, pulling it up, then rested his lips on Carolyn's dewy forehead.

Neither spoke as the last ripples of what had been great waves of release whispered throughout them, then stilled.

"Oh-h-h, my," Carolyn said finally.

"I know. I have never in my life..." His voice trailed off as he realized he did not have the words to describe what had just transpired between them.

The sweet bliss of sleep began to creep over Ryan, and he struggled to stay awake.

"Fading fast. I'd better leave before I'm dead to the world."

"You don't have to go. Unless you want to."

"No, I want to wake up next to you in the morning, Carolyn."

"Then stay with me, Ryan. Knowing you'll be here at dawn's light is perfect. Everything is just perfect." Even *she* knew with a womanly wisdom she hadn't known she possessed that what they had shared was rare and very, very special.

"Mmm," he said, as he began to give up his battle against the sleep that beckoned. "Perfect."

Except, he thought foggily, what about the secrets?

Hers. His.

Which kept this glorious night just a step away from being perfect.

Don't think, Sharpe, he told himself. Not now. Don't diminish the incredible lovemaking shared with Carolyn. Just...go...to...sleep.

Carolyn lay unmoving next to Ryan, waiting until his breathing became slow and steady, indicating he had given way to the oblivion of sleep.

Then carefully, so carefully, she eased away from him, her gaze riveted on his face to be certain she didn't waken him. Sitting up she removed her hearing aids, slipped them into the drawer of the nightstand next to the bed, then snapped off the light.

Returning to Ryan's side, she closed her eyes and with one hand resting on his chest to feel the beat of his heart, Carolyn slept.

The next morning Ryan stood next to the bed clad only in his jeans and holding a tray. He smiled as he watched Carolyn sleep. She was on her stomach, one leg slightly bent, one arm wrapped around the pillow where her head was snuggled. She reminded him of a little girl sprawled on her tummy in slumber after a hard day's play.

But Carolyn St. John, he thought in the next instant, was *not* a little girl. She was most definitely a woman. When they had made love, she'd given of herself freely, holding nothing back. She had shared equally in the intimate act that was as ancient as time itself, yet last night it had seemed as though it had been created only for them.

As the sensual mist began to creep over Ryan again, he blinked, shook his head slightly and cleared his throat.

"Rise and shine, my lovely," he said. "I've made you a breakfast fit for a queen."

Carolyn didn't stir.

"Carolyn? Hey, sleepyhead, are you in there? Your coffee is getting cold."

Carolyn still didn't move.

Ryan set the tray on the nightstand and jiggled Carolyn's shoulder. She jerked, rolled over and stared at him with wide eyes.

"Wow," he said, smiling. "You sleep like a dead person. I didn't mean to startle you like that, but I come bearing the gift of your breakfast."

Chilling panic rushed through Carolyn as she focused intently on Ryan's mouth, reading his lips.

She hadn't thought this through, her mind yelled. She'd just naively believed she'd wake before Ryan, insert her hearing aids and... Calm down, Carolyn.

"What a lovely surprise," she said.

She pushed her pillow behind her, sat up, then grabbed the sheet to cover her bare breasts, and tucked the material around her.

"Breakfast in bed? I could get used to being spoiled like this."

Ryan set the tray on her lap.

"Aren't you having any?"

"I ate as I cooked."

Carolyn picked up the mug of steaming coffee, took a sip, then wrinkled her nose.

"I hate to be picky since I'm being waited on hand and foot, but could you please, please, add just a tad more sugar to this?"

Ryan bowed from the waist. "I live to serve, madam." He took the mug and headed for the doorway. "I'll be right back."

With trembling hands, Carolyn opened the drawer to the nightstand and snatched up the hearing aids. She inserted one, fumbled with the other, then managed to get it into place just as Ryan reentered the bedroom.

"Try that," he said, handing her the mug of coffee. "If it's not right yet, just say so."

Carolyn took a swallow. "Excellent. Thank you so much, Ryan, for going to all this fuss. I feel very pampered and special."

"Everyone should be pampered once in a while," he said, sitting on the bed just beyond her feet. "And you *are* special, no doubt about it. I made you another omelet, due to the fact that was all I could produce from what I found in your refrigerator.''

''Well, I've already confessed that I'm not into cooking,'' she said, then took a bite of the fluffy omelet. ''Mmm.''

''It passes the test?''

''Mmm,'' she said, nodding.

''Good. Okay, you eat that while I shower. I didn't want to wake you by running the water.'' Ryan chuckled. ''But now I know that Niagara Falls could take up residency in your bathroom and you'd sleep right through its arrival.'' He got to his feet. ''I shall return. Oh, and I promise not to use all the hot water.''

''What a guy.''

''Awesome, isn't it?'' he said, then disappeared into the bathroom and shut the door.

Carolyn's shoulders slumped and she closed her eyes for a long moment, drawing several deep, steadying breaths.

Secrets kept have the power to destroy.

The words Margaret MacAllister had spoken yesterday suddenly hammered against Carolyn's mind, and a shiver coursed through her.

No, Carolyn thought, forcing herself to take another bite of breakfast. That wasn't true in this case. Her secret *told* had the power to destroy. And as she had said to Margaret, she just wasn't prepared to end what she was sharing with Ryan. Not yet.

The sound of the water in the shower stopped, and Carolyn took several quick bites of the omelet without really tasting it. She was nibbling on the piece of toast when Ryan opened the bathroom door, a cloud of soapy-smelling steam wafting into the room. Ryan emerged with a towel wrapped around his hips.

"I borrowed your cute little pink razor," he said, running one hand over his chin. "I think I cut myself forty-two times."

Carolyn laughed. "There is a package of new razors under the sink in there. They are, however, all cute and pink."

Ryan dropped the towel to the floor and began to dress, causing Carolyn's hand to still with the coffee mug halfway to her mouth as she watched him.

Magnificent, she thought. Ryan was so beautifully proportioned, each part of his body flowing naturally into the next.

When Ryan glanced at her, she took a swallow of coffee, then coughed.

"I saw you peeking." He smiled. "Did you enjoy my reverse striptease?"

Carolyn batted her eyelashes. "Pardon me? I have no idea as to what you are referring, sir."

"Oh, okay," he said, chuckling.

Ryan returned the towel to bathroom, then came around the bed and sat down again just beyond Carolyn's feet.

"How's the breakfast?"

"Delicious. Thank you again."

"Sure." Ryan paused. "I was thinking while I was in the shower. I'm one of those guys who does heavy-duty mind stuff underwater."

"Ah," Carolyn said nodding, then drained the coffee mug and set it on the tray.

"Anyway, while I was doing my fish thing," Ryan went on, "I came up with a plan for today, and I want to run it by you.

"I'd like to try to connect with Patty this morning if I can. She's been acting strange lately, and I told my dad yesterday that I'd talk to her, see if I can get her to open up about what's wrong."

"Patty," Carolyn said, frowning. "I don't remember meeting her yesterday."

"That's because she wasn't there," he said, running one hand over the back of his neck. "She didn't attend very many of the family gatherings during the holidays, came up with rather lame excuses at the last minute for why they couldn't come.

"When she did show up, it was just with my nephew, Tucker—he's two. He's part kangaroo, I think. He just bounces all over the place, never seems to run out of energy. Dynamite kid, really cute and...

"I'm getting off the subject. Looking back over the holidays I realize we didn't see Peter, Patty's husband, at all. My folks are worried about Patty, are afraid that she and Peter might be having marital problems, but don't want to intrude on their privacy. My dad thought Patty might talk to me because we've always been very close."

"Instead of her feeling like a child running home to mommy and daddy to spill out her woes."

"Yes, exactly," Ryan said, a touch of awe in his voice. "You got it in one. You're a very perceptive, sensitive woman, Carolyn."

"Oh, I don't know about that," she said, shrugging. "It just makes sense to me, that's all. Past a certain age, I think, we begin to want to protect our parents from our troubles, problems, work them out on our own. Or as in Patty's case, confide in a loving brother. She's very fortunate to have you."

"As an only child, who do you talk to when you're upset, have a rotten hand to deal with?"

"No one. I speak with my parents every week on the phone and tell them that I'm fine, even if I'm not. But this conversation isn't about me, Ryan. We're discussing your sister."

Ryan looked at her for another long, intense moment, then nodded.

"I'll call Patty from here and see if maybe Peter is off playing golf or whatever so I can get her alone. Then I thought maybe you and I might go to the movies this afternoon, unless you'd rather spend a lazy Sunday and go to a flick..."

Don't do it, Sharpe, he told himself. Why set himself up to be popped in the chops. Don't push on the subject of Carolyn's secretive Monday night.

"...tomorrow night," he finished. So much for listening to his own words of wisdom.

"I...I can't tomorrow night," Carolyn said, setting the tray next to her on the bed.

A cold, painful knot tightened in Ryan's stomach. "Right. Well, so be it."

"But I'd like to see a movie this afternoon. I'm off to the shower. You can use the phone here next to the bed to call your sister."

Ryan reached over and retrieved the tray, then Carolyn scooted across the bed and disappeared into the bathroom, closing the door behind her.

"Where do you go on Monday night, Carolyn St. John?" Ryan said, staring at the door. "Ah, hell, why did I do that to myself? Just had to test it out again, didn't you, Sharpe? Cripe."

He set the tray on the floor, snatched up the

receiver to the telephone and pushed the buttons to call Patty.

Patty was home and, while she was reluctant at first to agree to Ryan's request to drop by, stating she had mounds of laundry to do, she finally said she would see him.

When Carolyn emerged from the bathroom clad in a terry-cloth robe and a towel wrapped around her freshly shampooed hair, Ryan swept her into his arms and kissed her. The kiss was so intense, so passionate, that when he released her she had to sink onto the edge of the bed as her trembling legs refused to support her.

"Hold that thought," he said, his voice gritty with desire. "I'm going to my place to change into fresh clothes, then over to Patty's. I'll be back here sometime this afternoon."

"Works for me," Carolyn said, then pointed one finger in the air. "I must say, when you kiss a person, you really…kiss a person."

"You're no slouch in that department, either," Ryan said, drawing one thumb over Carolyn's lips. "Oh, man, I'm outta here before I can't stand the thought of being outta here. 'Bye."

"'Bye," Carolyn said dreamily, as Ryan strode from the room.

She sat there staring into space, reliving every exquisite memorized moment of her night with

Ryan, then finally told herself to get it in gear or she'd still be in her bathrobe when Ryan returned.

She dressed in jeans and a blue sweater with white snowflakes, then made the bed, stopping to pick up the pillow where Ryan had laid his head. She pressed the pillow to her face, inhaling and savoring his lingering aroma.

Laughing merrily, she decided that had been a rather childish thing to do and knew she didn't give a rip. She was thoroughly enjoying every bit of evidence that Ryan had spent the night there, including the soggy towel draped over the bar in the bathroom.

She telephoned her parents, chattered on about this and that, including the heartwarming story of Kimiko Sung. She did not, however, say one word about Ryan Sharpe.

There was no point in telling her parents about Ryan, Carolyn thought, her hand still on the telephone receiver after she hung up. They would only worry that she was unhappy when she informed them later that Ryan was no longer a part of her life. They wouldn't quite believe that she was fine because she had known all along that what she was sharing with Ryan was temporary.

Carolyn left the bedroom and went down the hall to the living room. She sat on the sofa, got up again, then plunked back down.

This was just great, she thought with self-disgust. She never had a problem filling her idle hours, yet here she was feeling restless and edgy, listening for the sound of Ryan's knock at the door.

"Get a grip, Carolyn St. John," she said aloud. "Do something productive."

She marched into the kitchen and ate six chocolate chip cookies.

The following hours dragged by. Carolyn washed the kitchen floor, which didn't need washing. Dusted furniture that didn't need dusting. Rearranged her closet, then put everything back where it had been in the first place. Attempted and failed to lose herself in a novel. Then stretched out on the sofa in defeat, stared at the ceiling and waited for Ryan.

Just after six o'clock that evening the long-awaited knock sounded at the door. Carolyn rushed across the room and threw open the door, her eyes widening as she stared at Ryan. He looked completely exhausted, his hair was tousled as though he'd been continually dragging his hands through it, and the warm glow of his skin had been replaced with a nearly gray pallor.

"Come in." She stepped back, then closed the door behind him when he entered. "What's wrong? You look just awful."

Ryan reached for her, pulling her into a tight

embrace and burying his face in her silky hair. She felt a tremor shudder through him, then he released her. Holding fast to one of her hands, he went to the sofa and sank onto it heavily with Carolyn in tow. She shifted slightly so she could look directly at him.

"Ryan?"

"I'm sorry I was gone so long," he said, staring at a spot on the far wall. "I should have called, but the whole thing was such a mess and…" He shook his head.

"What whole thing was a mess? Has something happened to Patty? Her baby? Husband? Ryan, please, talk to me."

"Oh, yeah, something has happened to Patty," he said, lunging to his feet and beginning to pace. "Peter, her husband, the wonderful Peter Clark, left Patty and Tucker the day after Thanksgiving and moved in with his secretary from the insurance company where he works."

"Oh, my gosh," Carolyn said, her hands flying to her cheeks.

Ryan continued his trek around the room, shoving one hand through his hair every few feet.

"It gets worse. Peter served Patty with divorce papers a week before Christmas. Can you believe that scum?"

"And none of you knew? Patty didn't tell anyone?"

Ryan slouched back onto the sofa and sighed. "No, she didn't tell a soul. She said she was numb at first, couldn't believe it, was sure Peter would come to his senses and return home.

"Then when it really sank in, she was determined not to ruin the family's holidays with such devastating news. That explains why she didn't come to most of the gatherings we had, and when she did show up, it was just her and Tucker. She made lame excuses for Peter."

"But she told you the truth when you went to see her today?"

"Not at first. Not until I pushed her. And guess where her head is now? She blames herself for Peter taking a hike. If she'd been a better wife, kept a neater house, prepared more elaborate meals when Peter came home from a hard day at work. On the list goes. She's been hiding out in that house, beating herself up emotionally for what that louse did to her and to Tucker."

"But Peter was cheating on her. Oh, Ryan, she mustn't blame herself like this. If Peter was unhappy they could have gone for counseling or something. Poor Patty. My heart just aches for her."

"Peter would be aching if I got my hands on

him," Ryan said, narrowing his eyes. "I'd like nothing better than to clean his clock."

"That wouldn't change anything. What did you do, say to her?"

"She finally fell apart. Ah, Carolyn, she cried so hard, so long, as though her heart was shattering into a million pieces. She needed to cry, I know that, but it just ripped me up. I convinced her that it was time to reach out to the family who loves her, and she didn't have the energy to argue with me. I called our parents, and they came right over, then I phoned Jessica, and she came, too. Jessica is going to be Patty's attorney through the divorce."

Carolyn nodded.

"And I kept the best till last, Carolyn," Ryan said, a rough edge to his voice. "Patty just found out that she's pregnant. She told Peter, and he just said to contact his attorney."

"Oh, my God," Carolyn whispered.

"Patty's world has fallen apart. Tucker's world has fallen apart. He senses something is wrong and is acting out a lot. And now there's another baby on the way whose world fell apart before he or she could even be born.

"Why? Because that damn Peter is a sleazeball. Was he up-front with Patty? Did he tell her the truth? Say he didn't love her anymore and wanted out of their marriage? Oh, no, not the stud. He carried on a cheap affair behind her back for heaven only knows how long. He came home at night, ate dinner with his wife and son, slept in his marriage bed and the whole damn time Peter Clark was harboring a secret.

"A secret that has devastated my sister. There's no excuse for what he's done. None. That secret of Peter's has buried Patty under the rubble of what she had and is now gone forever."

Ryan looked directly at Carolyn, and her breath caught as she saw the fury and pain in his dark eyes.

"It's a small word, isn't it?" he said, his voice raspy with emotion. "Secret. Just six little letters. Yet it has the power to destroy, power beyond measure. I despise that word, Carolyn. *Secret. I hate it.*"

Carolyn felt the color drain from her face and her hands fluttered up toward her ears, before she realized they had moved. She nodded jerkily, then clasped her hands tightly in her lap.

"I understand why you feel that way," she said, averting her eyes from Ryan's. "You have just cause because of what has happened to Patty. But sometimes there are sound reasons why a person keeps a secret, is silent about something that—"

"No," Ryan said, slicing one hand through the air.

"All right. This obviously isn't the time to discuss this, not when you're focused on what Peter's secret did to your sister and nephew." She paused. "You're exhausted, Ryan, emotionally drained. Have you eaten? Shall I fix you something?"

"I'm not hungry. Ah, Carolyn, I'm wiped out, and I'm definitely not good company. I need to be alone, try to digest all of this, hopefully come up with some way I can help Patty."

"Just love her, be there for her."

"Yeah," Ryan said, then got to his feet. "I'm going to head on home. I'm sorry about today, our plans."

Carolyn stood. "Don't worry about that. Try to get some rest if you can."

Ryan nodded, brushed his lips over Carolyn's and headed for the door. He stopped with his hand on the doorknob and looked back at her.

"Thank you for being so understanding. For letting me dump all over you. For being here for me. You're a very special lady, Carolyn, and it's no *secret* that I care about you very much." He laughed, the sound sharp and edgy, holding no real humor. "*Secret.* God, I hate that word. I'll talk to you soon."

"Yes, fine," Carolyn said, then wrapped her hands around her elbows.

Ryan left the apartment, but Carolyn continued to stand where she was for several long agonizing minutes. Then tears filled her eyes as she lifted trembling hands to cover her ears.

The secret she was keeping from Ryan had suddenly grown in magnitude, because he now hated the very idea of secrets.

But what of the secrets that Ryan was harboring? Didn't he realize that he was guilty of keeping important things from her? Or did he view his private demons as just that—private? Did he even consider that she should know what had caused his inner pain? Or didn't she play an important enough role in his life?

Chapter Nine

The next morning when Carolyn arrived at work, she sank into the chair behind her desk, rested her head back on the top of the chair and closed her eyes.

She was exhausted, she thought, and the day had hardly begun. She'd had only snatches of sleep last night.

Janice came rushing into the office, causing Carolyn to jerk in surprise at the sudden intrusion.

"Thank goodness you're here," Janice said, taking a chair opposite Carolyn's desk. "This is awful, so sad and terrible, and now everything is a complicated tangle and…"

"Halt," Carolyn said, leaning forward. "Take a deep breath, calm down and tell me what's wrong."

"Okay," Janice said, drawing a steadying breath. "Elizabeth is gone, poof, winging her way to the Philippines for the International Adoption Conference."

"Yes," Carolyn said, nodding. "I'm temporarily in charge here."

"Right, and Kimiko Sung arrives from Korea this afternoon. Well, the teenage son of Kimiko's host family was in an automobile accident last night."

"What?" Carolyn said, her eyes widening.

"He just got his driver's license and...he's got a broken leg and arm and a concussion. The family is camped out at the hospital. Carolyn, they can't take on the care for Kimiko now, they just can't."

"No, no, of course they can't," Carolyn said, her mind racing. "He's going to be all right, isn't he? The host family's son?"

"Yes, in time, but he's all banged up and he needs his family's support. Carolyn, someone else has got to step in and take care of Kimiko. That someone is you."

"Me?" Carolyn said, nearly shrieking. "But, Janice, that's not possible. I have a spare bedroom in my apartment, but all that's in there is some bookcases and a computer. I don't even have a place for Kimiko to sleep.

"Plus, I know nothing about taking care of children. I just don't. I mean, I've always believed that I would be a good mother if I had a baby, but this is an entirely different set of circumstances.

"Not only that, but the host family took courses in speaking Korean. I wouldn't even be able to communicate with that frightened little boy."

"There's no one else to do it," Janice said, jumping to her feet. "Think about our staff, Carolyn. I live in an apartment with three roommates. It's bedlam.

"Three of the men here are bachelors who have zip experience with kids. They sure know how to do their jobs, but take that little guy home? Not a chance.

"The other women are either single with no hands-on time with children, or they're overflowing with kids at home, or they're grandmothers who just don't have the energy to care for Kimiko."

"Did you hear what *I* said? I'm an only child. I never baby-sat when I was growing up. I love it when our families bring the little ones into the office to visit us, but I'd panic if one of them asked me to watch their new darling while they ran an errand or whatever. I am..."

"In charge of this agency at the moment," Janice said. "That means the buck stops with you, or in this case, one scared to death five-year-old is all yours. I'll get you the flight number of his plane and his time of arrival. You're going to have to do this, Carolyn. There just isn't anyone else."

"Oh…my…God," Carolyn said, sinking back in her chair. "I don't believe this."

"Believe it. I think maybe you should go rent a bed or cot or something for Kimiko to sleep on at your apartment."

"But what do I feed him?"

"Hey, I don't know what five-year-old American kids eat, let alone one from Korea. Hamburgers and fries? Doesn't every country in the world have hamburgers and fries?" She threw up her hands. "I don't have a clue." She stomped out of the office.

"Ryan will know what Kimiko eats," Carolyn said aloud, snatching up the receiver to the telephone. In the next instant she replaced it with a sigh. "No."

No, she thought, Ryan has his own problems on this bleak Monday morning. He probably hadn't slept any better than she had because of being upset about Patty.

She was just going to have to tackle this situation on her own and she would. But it sure would help if she knew where to begin. Oh, poor Kimiko. He deserved better than this, but he was stuck with her.

"A bed," she said, getting to her feet. "I must get that little guy something to sleep on. Toys. He'll need toys to play with. Food. Oh, for heaven's sake, Kimiko has probably never seen a hamburger with fries before in his life."

At seven o'clock that evening Kimiko Sung and Carolyn St. John were both in tears.

Kimiko was huddled in the corner of the living room, his legs drawn up and encircled with his arms, his face buried in his knees as he cried.

Carolyn was sitting on the floor in front of him, unable to stop the flow of her own tears of fatigue, a deep feeling of helplessness and an aching heart for the unhappy child.

Kimiko tightened his hold on his legs as Carolyn placed a trembling hand gently on the top of his head, his dark hair sweaty from crying for what seemed an eternity. She snatched her hand back as she felt him cringe at her touch, and more tears spilled onto her pale cheeks.

"Oh, sweetie, don't cry," she said, sniffling. "You're so tired, and you must be hungry. I'm so sorry you didn't like the hamburger and fries, or the toys, or... Oh, Kimiko, I just don't know what to do for you.''

Think, Carolyn, she ordered herself, dashing the tears from her face. Stop wailing and think. Kimiko was so scared. She couldn't sooth his fears because she didn't know one word of Korean, like—

Carolyn scrambled to her feet, her heart racing.

''Like Ryan does,'' she said, dashing across the room to the telephone.

She lifted the receiver, swallowed a sob as she realized she didn't know Ryan's number, then pulled the telephone book out of the drawer of the end table and flipped through the pages.

''Sharpe, Sharpe, Sharpe,'' she said, running a fingertip down the *S* page. ''There it is. Okay. Get a grip, Carolyn.''

She pressed the numbers and heard the ringing on the other end.

''Please be there, Ryan,'' she whispered. ''Please, please, please be home.''

''Hello?'' a deep voice said.

''Ryan?'' Carolyn said, sinking onto the edge of the sofa. ''Oh, thank God.''

''Carolyn?'' Ryan said. ''What's wrong? Are you crying? Carolyn?''

''Oh, Ryan,'' she said, failing to stem the fresh flow of tears. ''It's Kimiko. The host family couldn't take him because their son was in an accident, so I picked him up at the airport and brought him here and rented a bed for him and bought him some toys and offered him a hamburger and fries, and he's just crying and crying, and it's just breaking my heart because he's so sad and scared, and I don't know what to do for him and...Ryan, please, I need you.''

''I'm on my way.''

''Oh, Ryan, thank you so much. I—'' Carolyn stopped speaking as she realized that the dial tone was buzzing in her ear.

''Oh, thank you, thank you,'' she rambled on as she replaced the receiver. ''I love you, Ryan. No, I don't. That's just popped out of my mouth because I'm a total wreck so it doesn't count, and I'm glad you hung up before you heard me say that because that would be the last straw and I don't have room for one more straw and...oh-h-h.''

Carolyn got to her feet and began to pace, looking at the door, willing it to echo the sound of Ryan's knock, then shifting her gaze to the tiny boy in the corner who was still sobbing, which caused her to match him tear for tear.

After what seemed like forever, a sharp rap came at the door. Carolyn ran to open the door, then flung herself into Ryan's arms before he could even enter the apartment.

"Hey," he said, holding her close. "Take it easy, sweetheart. May I come in?"

Carolyn nodded jerkily and stepped out of Ryan's embrace. He came into the living room, closed the door, then gripped Carolyn's shoulders.

"Oh, man, look at you. Why didn't you call me sooner?"

"Because...because," Carolyn said, then a sob caught in her throat, "I knew you were already upset about Patty, and I didn't want to bother you with my problems, but that poor baby over there is so scared, so sad, and..."

"Okay, okay," Ryan said. "You sit down on the sofa and take a deep breath." He led her forward and settled her onto the cushion. "Stay."

"Roll over, play dead, fetch," Carolyn said, with a hysterical-sounding giggle.

"Whatever works. You just sit there and concentrate on pulling yourself together. You're going to have a doozy of a sinus headache if you don't stop crying."

"I look awful when I cry," Carolyn said, sniffling.

"Yep, you're a mess," Ryan said, taking a clean white handkerchief from his back pocket. "Here. Blow your nose or something while I see if I can figure out Kimiko's problem." He glanced at the child. "He sure is small for his age, isn't he?"

"He's scared, Ryan," Carolyn said, pressing the handkerchief to her nose, "and he must be hungry, but he's terrified of me, doesn't want me to touch him or..."

"Whoa," Ryan said. "One thing at a time here."

"Thank you, Ryan. I needed you and you came. That means so much to me." Carolyn shook her head. "You must feel like you're dealing with *two* weeping children here. Forget about me. Please try to help Kimiko."

"Yep."

Ryan crossed the room, hunkered down in front of the five-year-old bundle and began to speak Korean to him in a soft voice that immediately had a soothing effect on Carolyn even though she had no idea what Ryan was saying.

Kimiko lifted his head slowly and stared at Ryan, who continued to talk to him. Kimiko said something in a tiny tearful voice, and Ryan nodded, then spoke to him again.

The conversation went on for several minutes, then Carolyn's breath caught as Kimiko lunged to his feet, threw his arms around Ryan's neck and buried his face in Ryan's shoulder. Ryan got to his feet with Kimiko in his arms, rubbing the child's back in a gentle motion.

"Easy does it, kiddo," Ryan said. "Everything

is going to be just fine. First thing on the agenda is a trip to the bathroom.''

''I showed him the bathroom, but he just shrieked and ran back to his spot against the wall.''

''He may never have seen an indoor bathroom before,'' Ryan said, starting across the room. ''You said his parents couldn't afford the surgery he needs. He very likely lives in a pretty primitive village with no modern conveniences. We shall return, Carolyn.''

Oh, look at them, Carolyn thought, as Ryan disappeared from view with Kimiko held tightly in his arms. What a beautiful picture they made. The big, strong father comforting the frightened son, calming his fears, making everything all right. Ryan would be such a marvelous daddy, the type of man who would always be there for his children and his…his wife.

Ryan returned to the living room with Kimiko walking beside him, Kimiko's little hand tightly grasping Ryan's fingers.

''Next up,'' Ryan said, chuckling, ''is the matter of your trying to put blood on his biscuit.''

Carolyn got to her feet. ''I did what?'' Her eyes widened. ''Oh, my gosh. I put ketchup on his hamburger. No wonder he's scared to death of me. He must think I'm some kind of monster.''

''Don't worry about it,'' Ryan said. ''I'm going

to scramble him an egg. You can make him some toast with butter. Okay? And pour him a glass of milk?''

''Yes. Yes, of course.''

A short time later Kimiko was shoveling in spoonfuls of scrambled egg, prompting Ryan to say something to him in Korean that resulted in the little boy slowing down his consumption of the food. Ryan and Carolyn stood next to the table, watching Kimiko eat.

''You know,'' Ryan said quietly, sliding his hands into the pockets of his slacks, ''this has been quite an experience. For the first time in my life I solved a problem, set things to rights because of who and what I am. My being different, per se, was exactly what was needed here tonight. It feels...'' He stopped speaking and cleared his throat as his emotions overcame him. ''It feels good, which definitely isn't a big enough word.''

''Oh, Ryan,'' Carolyn said, placing one hand on his arm. ''I don't know what Kimiko and I would have done without you tonight. I can't help but wonder if the parents who adopt older Asian children through the agency have problems like this and just didn't say anything to us about it.

''We tell the people who are adopting babies that they should dilute the formula they buy here when they first get home until the baby can tolerate how rich it is, compared to what we know they've been getting.

"But it never occurred to any of us that the older kids would be offered foods they'd never seen or tasted before. There have probably been upset tummies that have been chalked up to adjusting to their new home and the strangers around them.

"Because of what you've taught me tonight I now know this is something we need to address at the agency. I owe you so many thank-yous the list is getting ridiculously long. Because of your background you have knowledge that will smooth rough waters for these scared little guys in the future."

"I can help because of my heritage," Ryan said, shaking his head. "Like I said, this is definitely a new experience for me."

"A warm fuzzy feeling?" Carolyn said, smiling.

"In spades," he said, matching her smile.

Carolyn shifted her gaze to Kimiko. "Isn't he a beautiful child? His hair is so silky and his eyes seem to possess the ability to see right into a person's soul, just like yours do. They're so dark, so compelling."

"So Asian," Ryan said, frowning. "Just like my eyes are."

Carolyn looked up at Ryan again. "I think you have the most gorgeous eyes I've ever seen."

Ryan turned his head to meet Carolyn's gaze. "You do? I mean, hey, they shout the message, you know? Yo, attention everyone, this guy is different."

"This guy is special, unique and wonderful." Carolyn smiled. "That makes you different big time, because a great many men I've met are real jerks."

Ryan laughed, then quieted as Kimiko spoke.

"He wants another egg," he said, picking up Kimiko's plate.

"I'm glad to see him eating so well. He's so thin, and there's an unhealthy pallor beneath his skin tone."

"Well, I imagine his medical problem has taken a toll," Ryan said, going back to the stove. "Once they fix that hole in his heart I bet that he'll start to fill out, grow bigger, be a hustlin' bustlin' little boy like any other five-year-old."

"Yes," Carolyn said, nodding. "If only all physical impairments could be solved by a team of doctor performing surgery and... Oh, good heavens. Physical impairments. This is Monday night. I've got to call and explain why I didn't show up to teach my class." She turned and started from the room.

"You teach a class on Monday nights? What kind of class?"

"Sign language," she said, as she hurried away.

Ryan finished preparing Kimiko's egg by rote, his mind racing.

That was where Carolyn went every Monday night? he thought, placing the plate back in front of Kimiko. She taught a sign language class? Why was she so proficient in sign language? Well, it probably fascinated her at some point and she got so good at it she was capable of teaching it to other people.

But why the secrecy about it, the way she skittered around saying where she was going on Monday nights? Did that make sense? Hell no, not even close. Why hadn't she just said that she couldn't see him on Monday nights because she taught a class in sign language? Well, there was only one way to find out. Ask her. And he would, just as soon as they got Kimiko settled into bed.

Carolyn returned to the kitchen, and Ryan had to nearly bite his tongue to keep from broaching the subject. He looked at her for a long moment, willing her to offer some explanation.

"If Kimiko hasn't seen a bathroom before, how do you think he'll feel about taking a bath?"

Ryan inwardly sighed. So that was how she was going to play it. Pretend that her revelation about teaching sign language had never happened. Damn.

"Do you think you can explain a bath to Kimiko, Ryan?"

"I'll give it my best shot."

Think about little boys and bubble baths, Ryan, Carolyn mentally pleaded. Please forget what you heard me say earlier. Oh, she couldn't believe she'd just opened her mouth and said it. She was definitely an overloaded wreck.

Ryan sat down across from Kimiko, and a conversation in Korean took place between the pair. Kimiko frowned, shook his head, then finally nodded.

"The bath is a go," Ryan said to Carolyn. "What kind of clothes did he bring with him?"

"Not many. He just has a small tote made of what looks like carpet scraps with a few things to wear. I bought him a plastic dump truck, a coloring book, and crayons and a storybook before I picked him up. It didn't occur to me that he would need clothes."

"Well, we can remedy that tomorrow. Where is he going to sleep?"

"I rented a bed and had it delivered. It's in the spare bedroom where I keep my computer."

"Okay," Ryan said, getting to his feet. "I'll go give him a bath, then we'll sit together by his bed while I attempt to translate the gist of the story in the book you got him. That way he'll start to realize that you're not a scary lady who does nothing more than try to put blood on his biscuit.''

"I feel so bad about that," Carolyn said, shaking her head. "It's a prime example of how things can be so misconstrued by someone who doesn't understand what's going on."

"There's a lot of that going around," Ryan said, looking at her intently. "Come on, Kimiko," he said, shifting his gaze back to the little boy. "Let's hit the suds."

"I'll clean the kitchen while you're giving him a bath. Call me when you're ready to read to him, or tell him the story or however you think you'll be able to do it."

"Right," Ryan said gruffly, then swung Kimiko up into his arms and left the kitchen.

Carolyn sighed as a wave of total exhaustion swept through her.

Maybe, she thought, as she began the kitchen chores, Ryan wouldn't push tonight for answers, due to the fact that they were focusing on Kimiko. Maybe, just maybe, he'd put the whole thing on the back burner for now, making it possible for her to discuss it calmly and coolly when she wasn't so very, very tired.

There was a slim chance of that happening, but she was going to hang on to the slender thread of hope like a lifeline.

Carolyn finished cleaning, then went through her bedroom to stand at the open doorway to the bathroom, a smile instantly forming on her lips as she savored the sound of Ryan's laughter intertwining with Kimiko's.

The bathtub held an enormous mound of bubbles that Kimiko was throwing in the air by the handful. Ryan was sitting on the mat on the floor, poking bubbles that escaped beyond the rim of the tub.

The now-familiar warmth tiptoed around Carolyn's heart as she looked at the pair, and she reaffirmed in her mind what a wonderful father Ryan would be.

"Okay, you're shivering. Time to rinse off, buddy. You've had a big day and you need some sleep, too."

"He doesn't have any pajamas. Why don't you put a pair of undies on him, and I'll get him one of my T-shirts to sleep in."

Ryan nodded, then pulled the plug in the bottom of the tub.

"Does he have tests, or something tomorrow at the hospital?" he said, standing Kimiko up in the tub and sluicing the bubbles off of him.

"Yes, at eleven in the morning. I have to take him to the office with me until it's time to keep his appointment. There are toys in the reception area at work he can play with…if he will.''

Ryan got to his feet, lifted Kimiko out of the tub and set him on the mat, then began to dry the little boy with a big, fluffy towel.

''Why don't I take him shopping for clothes instead? I'll come here in the morning and get him, then pick you up at your office, and the three of us will go to the hospital together.''

''Don't you have to work?''

''I'm on schedule with what I'm doing at the moment. I can spare the time.''

''Okay, thank you,'' Carolyn said. ''I'll get a T-shirt for Kimiko.''

A short time later Carolyn sat next to Ryan on the edge of Kimiko's bed and listened while Ryan spoke Korean as he turned the pages in the story-book. Kimiko's lashes drifted down, he popped his eyes open again, then gave up the battle and fell asleep.

Ryan closed the book and stared at Kimiko.

''He's such a neat little kid. Powerful, too. That tiny package has managed to wrap his fingers around my heart, and I don't think he's going to let go.''

''You're wonderful with him, Ryan,'' Carolyn said, her voice hushed. ''You're a natural-born father. A son of yours would look a great deal like Kimiko, too, I imagine.''

"A little bit maybe," Ryan said, his gaze still riveted on the sleeping child. "My American half would show up someplace, but my son would definitely have almond-shaped eyes. That Asian gene is obviously strong." He shook his head. "This is a crazy conversation. Let's get out of here before we wake him up."

Oh, let's not, Carolyn thought frantically. She'd much rather just sit there with Ryan and watch Kimiko sleep than go into the living room and run the risk of Ryan addressing the issue of the sign language classes.

Ryan got to his feet, went to the doorway, then turned to look at Carolyn where she was still sitting on the edge of the bed.

"Coming?" he said.

No, she thought.

"Yes," she said wearily.

Chapter Ten

When Carolyn stepped out of the room where Kimiko was now sleeping so peacefully, Ryan shut off the light and pulled the door half-closed. They went into the living room and Carolyn forced herself to smile.

"Goodness, I feel as though I've run a marathon or something." She paused. "Would you like a snack? You deserve a reward for being the hero to the rescue here tonight. I have some cookies and ice cream. I think there's some popcorn somewhere in a cupboard, too, or..."

"No, thank you," Ryan interrupted.

"Oh. Well, do you want to watch television?"

"Monday-night football, you mean?" Ryan said, looking directly at her. "The divisional eliminations are in progress, getting ready for the Super Bowl. That's what I usually do this time of year on Monday nights...watch the football game.

"But you may not even be aware that they play on Monday nights, Carolyn, because you have a standing engagement, don't you? You teach a sign language class."

Carolyn wrapped her hands around her elbows and lifted her chin.

"Yes, that's what I do every Monday night. I teach a free class at the community center for low-income families who have a hearing impaired child. I'm working with a darling little girl named Kendra."

"I see," Ryan said, folding his arms over his chest. "That's very admirable of you."

"It's extremely rewarding and I enjoy it very much. Wouldn't you like to sit down, Ryan?"

"No," he said, a deep frown knitting his brows. "What I would like, Carolyn, is an explanation as to why you didn't tell me that you teach sign language. Why is something like that a major, uh, here comes my favorite word...*secret* with you? Well?"

A rush of anger swept through Carolyn, but she

was just too exhausted to wonder where it had come from all of a sudden or to attempt to push it aside.

"Ah, yes," she said, an edge to her voice, "the subject of secrets. Tell me, Ryan, why haven't you shared...told me what happened to cause you such turmoil about your mixed heritage?

"You have secrets. I have secrets. It doesn't say much for the depth of our relationship, does it? But we don't want any depth, do we? What we have is temporary. I just didn't want it to end yet. Not yet."

"Wait just a damn minute here," Ryan said, his voice rising in volume. "Who's talking about ending our relationship?"

He looked quickly in the general direction of the room where Kimiko was sleeping and lowered his voice when he spoke again.

"All I'm saying, Carolyn, is that I'd like some answers to what I believe are very reasonable questions. As far as what happened to me in the past...there are just some things that are too painful to discuss."

"Oh, really?" Carolyn said, planting her hands on her hips. "I should bare my soul to you, lay it all out there for you despite how painful that might be for *me,* but you intend to keep your secrets? That's not how it works, Ryan. Not even close."

"For cripe's sake, Carolyn," Ryan said, dragging a restless hand through his hair. "You're comparing apples and oranges here. What happened to me is very personal, very rough to deal with. All I'm asking *you* is why didn't you tell me you teach that class on Monday night? It's a very simple question."

"No," Carolyn said quietly, "there's nothing simple about it, but my secrets are crushing me...they're just too heavy to deal with anymore. It's time you knew the truth."

She sank onto a chair and sighed in defeat.

This was it, she thought dismally. The end of what she had shared with this magnificent man. Oh, she didn't want this to happen. Not yet. Not yet.

"Would you please sit down, Ryan? What I'm about to tell you is going to take a while. I feel as though you're looming over me while I'm under a bare lightbulb."

"Whatever," Ryan muttered, then sat on the sofa, his arms spread along the top as he stared at Carolyn with a frown on his face.

Carolyn took a steadying breath and met Ryan's intense gaze.

"When I was three years old, I had meningitis which left me with...with impaired hearing. Months later I had yet another infection that diminished my hearing even more. My parents feared that future infections might render me totally deaf so we enrolled in sign language and lip-reading classes as a family. I thought the new games we were playing were great fun.''

Carolyn stopped speaking as memories of long ago swept before her mental vision. Ryan shifted forward, resting his elbows on his knees and making a steeple of his fingers which he rested lightly against his lips.

"Go on," he said.

"I'm not completely deaf," Carolyn continued, "but very close to it as I can only hear certain pitches of sound without my double hearing aids.

"That morning when you brought me breakfast in bed I didn't hear you, Ryan, because I'd taken out my hearing aids when you went to sleep. I read your lips, then inserted the hearing aids when you went to fix my coffee the way I'd asked you to."

"But..."

"Please," she said, raising one hand. "Let me finish. This is so difficult for me."

Ryan nodded.

"It was necessary for me to spend many years in speech therapy. Fortunately, I was talking when this first happened to me, but as my hearing diminished my speech was flat, not always clear, and therefore I had to be retrained to speak properly.

"I was teased at school about how I talked, but the therapist felt I would come along much quicker if I went to a regular school. It was a reasonable theory, I suppose, but those years were so harsh, so painful, and I became very shy and withdrawn.

"I wasn't like my classmates. I hated standing out. My self-esteem was very fragile, my self-confidence practically nonexistent. I have such wonderful, loving parents, but I was so young and I had to go off to that school each day…alone. I tried to be brave, didn't tell my parents I was upset but…"

"Carolyn…" Ryan said, then stopped speaking and shook his head.

"My speech was normal by the time I was in junior high, but I was still very shy and withdrawn. Later as an adult I focused on my studies at college, then on my career where I was accepted for my expertise. No one at the adoption agency knows that I wear hearing aids. I'm just me there, Carolyn St. John, who is very good at what I do. I'm not different.

"I haven't dated much because I have so many haunting ghosts from the past, so many insecurities and…I always seemed to be waiting to be rejected should a man discover my…my secret.

"And it happened. Several years ago I dated a man for quite some time and eventually told him

about my hearing aids because he didn't understand why I wouldn't attend sport events, live con-
certs, big parties with him. It was due to the noise
level, and I felt guilty for always having to come
up with an excuse for not going to those things
with him.''

"And?'' Ryan said, narrowing his eyes.

"He was furious, accused me of being a liar,
said I had no right to have kept something of this
magnitude from him for so many months. He said
I had presented myself as something that I really
wasn't. He ended our relationship right then, also
informing me that I'd better forget about ever being a mother because I wouldn't be able to hear
my own baby crying at night.''

"God,'' Ryan whispered.

"I knew he was wrong about that, about the
baby,'' Carolyn said, her voice trembling. "I know
I would be a good mother, a loving and devoted
mother. There are marvelous devices now like
flashing lights that will wake a sleeping mother
when her baby cries, but I didn't plead my case
with him. He'd rejected me because I was different, and there was nothing more to be said. I en-
visioned him always watching, waiting for me to
fall short because of my problem.

"I didn't date anyone for many months after

that. I just stayed home where it was safe. Later I went out occasionally but...

"Then I met you, Ryan. You were so persistent, as though you really wanted to be with me. You made me feel so special, womanly, feminine and pretty.

"I didn't have the courage to tell you about my hearing aids. I just told myself I'd have lovely memories to cherish when we were no longer together, because I knew that it was all temporary. I thought my handicap would cause it, us, to be over when I did finally confide in you. And now that time has come."

Carolyn drew a wobbly breath as she struggled against more tears that threatened. She clutched her hands in her lap and looked at them, not wanting to see whatever might be evident in Ryan's expressive eyes, on his face, as he processed all that she had told him.

Every muscle in Ryan's body was tensed to the point of pain as his mind raced. He replayed Carolyn's words in his mind like a recording, listening to them again, feeling them hammer relentlessly against his mind and heart, his very soul.

Carolyn honestly believed, he thought incredulously, as a chill swept through him, that he would have walked out of her life with a sense of disgust because she wore hearing aids. Didn't she trust and believe in him as a person, a man, enough to know that it wouldn't make the slightest difference to him? She had taken his measure and found him lacking, had in essence rejected him, deciding he wasn't worthy of knowing her secret.

He thought, truly believed, that what they had together was rare and more wonderful than anything he'd experienced before. But he was wrong.

Rejected, his mind screamed. Not good enough. Spurned. Just a man to have a good time with for a while, a temporary diversion from a narrow existence, but certainly not someone acceptable enough to know innermost secrets, or to be viewed in the long term. Too different. Not…good… enough as the man he was.

And, oh, God, it hurt.

He felt as though he was being ripped to shreds, could feel an achy sensation closing his throat that shouted to him that he was losing control of his emotions, might very well make a fool of himself by being unable to stop tears from filling his eyes.

He had to get out of here, he thought frantically. This was too big, too heavy—more than he could bear. He knew the pain of rejection. The cruel, cutting edge of it was familiar and detested.

But this wasn't the same. Was it? Carolyn wasn't rejecting him because of his heritage, his mixed blood. Yes, it was coming from a different place and...no, it wasn't, not really. No. God, it was all becoming a tangled maze in his mind, old ghosts rearing their ugly heads, confusing the facts of what was taking place now, but the bottom line was the same...

Rejected.

Ryan got to his feet, then staggered slightly as a wave of light-headedness swept over him. He steadied, focused on the door, then concentrated on placing one foot in front of the other as he crossed the room. He opened the door, hesitated, then left the apartment without looking back at Carolyn.

Carolyn sat statue still, hardly breathing, then finally rose and went to the sofa where she fluffed two throw pillows and set them back into place with jerky motions. She cocked her head to one side as she looked at the pillows, then switched them to the other end of the sofa.

She gathered the strewn crayons from the coffee table and placed each one carefully back in the box, being certain that the coveted red crayon was in the center of the front row.

The shades on the lamps on the end tables were given undivided attention, tilted a quarter of an inch to the left, the right, then back to the left.

And then she stopped in the middle of the room, wrapped her arms around her stomach and dropped to her knees, rocking back and forth as she sobbed openly, the tears running down her face and along her neck.

Ryan, her mind screamed. *No-o-o-o.*

She was crumbling, shattering into a million pieces, filled with an excruciating pain like nothing she had ever known.

Ryan had rejected her because she was different, so far, far away from being a normal woman. He hadn't hurled cruel and harsh words at her before walking out of her life. No. He had been so repulsed by her shortcomings, her hearing impairment, he couldn't even bear to speak to her after he'd learned the truth.

"It's okay," Carolyn whispered, a sob catching in her throat. "I knew what I had with Ryan was temporary. I knew. It's okay.

"It's over between us, finished, but it was just a matter of time until it was. But Ryan is gone. He's gone, and I miss him already. I'm so afraid that if I get in touch with myself, my heart, I might discover that I've fallen in love with him, which would mean I'll never be able to move past this pain, never be able to find all the pieces and put myself back together. Oh, God. *Ryan.*"

A shadow caught Carolyn's devastated and exhausted attention, and she jerked her head up to see Kimiko standing at the entrance to the living room. He was clutching the material of the front

of the baggy T-shirt tightly in his little hands, and
two tears slid slowly down his pale cheeks, followed by two more.

Carolyn opened her arms and extended them toward the little boy.

"Come here, sweet baby. I'll hold you. I'll hug
you. You're not alone, Kimiko. Don't be frightened, Kimiko Sung. I'm not a whole woman, but
that doesn't diminish the part of me that knows I
would be a good mother. It doesn't, Kimiko, I
swear it. Come to me and I'll chase all your fears
away."

Kimiko ran across the room and flung himself
into Carolyn's arms. She held him close, inhaling,
savoring, his wondrous aroma of soap, fresh air
and little boy as she buried her face in his dark,
silky hair.

She shifted around, then scooted backward to
rest against the sofa, Kimiko cradled in her lap and
clinging to her like a lifeline. He took one more
wobbly, tear-filled breath, then relaxed in her arms,
allowing sleep to once again take him to a world
of fairy-tale dreams that was waiting for children
to enter, where only they were allowed to go.

Carolyn stroked his hair with gentle fingertips,
then the soft skin of his cheek, and each tiny toe.
She left her own reality behind as she escaped, too,
indulged in a fantasy that this was the miracle, the

child, the son, created with Ryan Sharpe as they
made love in the private darkness of night.

She allowed herself that luxury, knowing it was
make-believe. But she gave it to herself like a precious gift wrapped in delicate tissue paper and
ready to be tucked away with other dreams that
would never come true.

Chapter Eleven

Early the next morning, Ryan stood in the corridor outside Carolyn's apartment, staring at the door. He lifted one hand to knock, then dropped it back to his side, shaking his head.

Taking a deep breath, he let it out slowly, puffing his cheeks, then rapped on the door. After what seemed like an eternity, Carolyn opened the door, an expression of surprise immediately evident on her face.

"Ryan?" Carolyn said. "What are you— I certainly didn't expect…"

"May I come in?" Ryan interrupted. "Please? I need to talk to you."

"Well, I..." Carolyn said, feeling the racing tempo of her heart. "Yes, I guess so."

As Ryan entered the apartment, Carolyn swept her gaze over him, savoring the sight of him, knowing she'd believed she'd never see him again.

Ryan looked awful, totally exhausted, she thought, closing the door. He had, like her, apparently not slept well. A scrutiny of her reflection in the mirror this morning had revealed dark smudges beneath her eyes and the lack of any healthy color on her cheeks. Ryan didn't appear to be in any better condition than she was.

Ryan waved at Kimiko who was sitting at the table eating his breakfast, then said something in Korean to the little boy. Kimiko smiled, nodded and answered Ryan in a chatter of words that Carolyn didn't understand.

"Kimiko likes you and you make good eggs," Ryan said, turning to face Carolyn. "I guess you've been forgiven for putting blood on his biscuit."

"Oh. Well. That's comforting." Carolyn wrapped her hands around her elbows. "Why are you here, Ryan? I really don't think we have anything further to say to each other, do you?"

"I'm so exhausted," Ryan said, frowning, "I

wouldn't know if there was something halfway intelligent in my muddled mess of a brain to say at this point."

"Then why are you here?"

"Because of Kimiko," he said. "He has a frightening ordeal to face, Carolyn, and I can hopefully ease some of his fears because I can communicate with him. I'd like to think that we're mature adults, can put aside the problems between us and concentrate on Kimiko."

"We don't have *problems,* Ryan," Carolyn said sharply. "That indicates a glitch in the program, something that can be corrected. Let's tell it like it is, shall we? There is *nothing* between us."

Except hurt, such deep and shattering pain, she thought. She felt the urge to fling herself into Ryan's arms, turn back the clock to before the devastating scene that had destroyed what they'd had together and kiss him until he couldn't breathe.

Ryan stared at the floor for a long moment, then met Carolyn's gaze again.

"Yeah, well, that's clear enough, isn't it?" he said, an edge to his voice. "Fine. What I'm asking is if you're willing to put Kimiko's needs front row center and allow me to be a part of what he's going through."

"Yes, of course. Kimiko is of primary importance. I'd appreciate any assistance you might give to make his ordeal easier. Perhaps you could meet us at the hospital later when I take him for the tests he's been scheduled for today.''

So cold, stilted, Ryan thought, and Carolyn was now speaking to a spot somewhere beyond his left shoulder, rather than look directly at him. He had the strange sensation that if he reached for her, he'd be able to actually feel the wall she'd built between them.

But then again that wall had always been there. He just hadn't been aware of it because he'd been so enchanted by Carolyn, so head over heels in…love with her? No, that was nuts. He really did need some sleep because he wasn't even close to thinking straight.

''What I'm proposing is that I still take Kimiko shopping for clothes this morning instead of his going to the office with you. We can connect with you later at the hospital.''

''He certainly needs clothes. His are clean and mended so carefully, but he has so few things. I have no idea if there are funds available. I just don't know the details of this program he's involved in. I'll need to check to see if there is money to purchase clothes.''

''I'll buy him whatever he needs. I want to.'' He attempted to produce a smile that failed to materialize. ''Hey, for all I know he's a relative of mine. Or whatever. Look, let me buy him some stuff. Okay? I asked Patty to help me out with the shopping because I thought it would do her good.''

Hopefully Patty was better at putting the broken pieces of her life back together than she was, Carolyn thought miserably.

''It's very thoughtful of you to be thinking of Patty as well as Kimiko. All right. I guess my only concern is that you keep a close eye on Kimiko to be certain that he doesn't get overtired at the malls.''

''Patty will know what to watch for in that arena. She's a good mother, a natural mother...like you, Carolyn.''

A sudden burst of laughter escaped from Carolyn's lips, surprising herself as much as it did Ryan.

''I don't think they hand out Mother of the Year Awards,'' she said, still smiling, ''to people who scare the bejeebers out of darling little boys.''

''Oh, that's right,'' Ryan said, matching her smile. ''I'm afraid you lose a point or two. I imagine you and I will chuckle about it whenever we're out together, stop for fast food and put ketchup on our hamburgers. We'll remember for a long time how Kimiko thought it was...'' Ryan's voice trailed off, and his smile faded. ''Well, that was a lame thing to say.''

"Yes, it was."

"Ah, Carolyn," Ryan said, lifting one hand toward her face. "I wish…"

"Ryan, don't," she whispered, "just don't. This is difficult enough. We're concentrating on Kimiko. There's no purpose to be served by rehashing it. I'd best go see if he's had enough breakfast."

Carolyn hurried across the room toward the kitchen area, telling herself that she did *not* feel a warmth on her cheek from where Ryan's hand had almost, but not quite, touched her skin. That imagined warmth was *not* now gaining power, turning into churning heat of desire that was swirling within her. She had *not* seen a flicker of want and need in the dark depths of Ryan's eyes, those compelling, mesmerizing eyes of his. No.

Ryan stood where he was, staring at the hand that had come within inches of Carolyn's cheek.

It was warm, tingling, he thought. It really was. The heat was sweeping up his arm and exploding throughout his body, coiling low, building to a painful ache of desire. Damn it.

This was going to be more difficult than he'd imagined. He'd thought that by concentrating on Kimiko, there wouldn't be room to dwell on what he had shared with Carolyn, how right and real and wonderful it had felt when he was with her, talking, laughing, making love.

He had to work on forgetting all of that, just remember how sliced and diced he'd been when he'd discovered that Carolyn didn't trust or believe in him enough to share her innermost secrets. Just remember that she had rejected him, focus on that pain.

But it was so difficult to accept that Carolyn believed that he would reject *her* because she was hearing impaired. Reject her? Hell, he respected her more than he would ever be able to put into words. She had faced a momentous challenge and won, accomplished her goals, was held in high regard in her chosen field. He was so proud of her, of what she had done, that he was rendered practically speechless with awe.

Maybe he should tell her that. No, what was the point? A great dissertation of compliments on his part wouldn't erase the bottom-line truth. He wouldn't even know about Carolyn wearing hearing aids if he hadn't pushed her for answers.

What they'd had together was over because he'd entered her private space, the distance she was determined to keep between them. Oh, sure, she felt he should divulge the painful memories of the rejection he'd suffered in the past, and she now stood in harsh judgment of him because he refused to do so.

Yes, sir, Ryan Sharpe, just bare your soul to the

lady as she was demanding, but don't expect her to return that gesture in kind. No way. There were very different rules in place for the goose and the gander.

But he'd forced her hand and she didn't like that, not one little bit. And so it was over. He hadn't followed the game plan and had been rejected and ejected.

Kimiko ran into the living room, pulling Ryan out of his tormenting thoughts. He swung the little boy up into his arms and tickled his tummy, savoring the sound of the laughter of the innocent.

"Does he have a sweater?" Ryan asked, looking at Carolyn where she stood by the kitchen table.

"No, just a lightweight cotton jacket."

"That should be okay. It's supposed to be fairly warm today. Okay, buddy, let's go. Where should I meet you at the hospital, Carolyn, and how close to eleven o'clock should I have him there?"

They settled on the time and place, Carolyn fetched Kimiko's jacket, then Ryan took the child's hand and started toward the door. Kimiko frowned and stopped, looking back at Carolyn.

"Oops," Ryan said. "I guess he thought you were coming with us."

"Tell him I'll see him later."

Ryan spoke to Kimiko in Korean, but he shook

his head and tugged his hand free of Ryan's to run to Carolyn and wrap his arms around her legs.

"Caro," Kimiko said.

"This could get dicey," Ryan said, frowning. "I sure don't want to drag him out of here kicking and screaming. You've won him over big time. Do you have any suggestions?"

"Use the universal code to the way to a male specimen's center of understanding. Tell him we'll be together to eat lunch."

Ryan chuckled. "I'll give it a try."

He spoke to Kimiko in Korean, and the little boy released his hold on Carolyn and looked up at her. She nodded, smiled, then leaned down and kissed him on the forehead. Kimiko turned, marched back to Ryan and took his hand.

"Like I said, you're a natural-born mother." His smile faded. "Your children will be very lucky little miracles, Carolyn."

"Thank you."

Their gazes met, and the distance between them seemed to disappear, despite the expanse of the room that separated them. Hearts began to thunder and heat began to churn within them.

A mist of sensuality encased them, bringing gentle memories of the wondrous hours they'd spent together, what they had shared, how much they had cared. They heard echoes of their laughter, then whispers of the other's name spoken reverently in passion-laden voices.

They were filled with a combination of the heat of desire plus the warmth of rightness, of being where they belonged—together.

"Ry," Kimiko said, wiggling Ryan's hand.

Ryan jerked at the sudden noise, and Carolyn took a sharp breath.

"Right," Ryan said, his voice sounding strange to his own ears. "We're outta here, kiddo. See you later, Carolyn. 'Bye."

Carolyn nodded, unable to speak as she realized she'd been holding her breath during the strange spell that had floated around and through her and Ryan, and had no air left to utter a single sound.

Ryan left the apartment quickly with Kimiko, then Carolyn sank onto a chair, her trembling legs refusing to hold her for another moment.

She wasn't going to survive this, she thought, pressing one hand to her flushed forehead. The next few days were going to be pure torture while she was in close proximity to Ryan Sharpe.

No, wait, she ordered herself. Get a grip. She'd focus on Ryan's rejection of her, of how he'd walked out of her apartment and her life without a backward glance or a single word once he learned she was hearing impaired. She'd remember the pain of that rejection, the tears that had flowed unchecked down her face, the sensation of her heart being smashed to smithereens.

"Got it," she said, getting to her feet and heading toward the kitchen to clean up from preparing Kimiko's breakfast. "I'm back in control, doing fine." She sighed. "I hope."

Several hours later Patty and Ryan sank onto a bench in a pretty little park.

"Oh-h-h, my feet are killing me," Patty said. "That was quite a shopping marathon. Kimiko is now one of the best-dressed kiddos in Ventura, and I'll bet you a buck that you'll have a battle on your hands when you try to get him to take off that new red baseball cap."

Patty reached over and squeezed Ryan's hand. "Thank you for inviting me and Tucker to come along with you and Kimiko, Ryan. I actually forgot about my woes for a while."

"That was the plan, sister mine," Ryan said, kissing her on the cheek. "Tucker and Kimiko are getting along very well. Boys and a ball. They're just sitting on the grass rolling it back and forth to each other and that's obviously major fun."

"Yep." Patty paused. "Would you care to tell me why you look as though you've been up all night?"

Ryan stretched his legs out in front of him and crossed them at the ankles.

"I just didn't sleep well," he said, directing his gaze toward where the boys were sitting on the grass. "It happens to everyone."

"To everyone who has something heavy on their mind. I'm not so centered on my own problems that I believe I'm the only one who has any. Is something wrong, Ryan?"

"No." Ryan sighed. "Yes. But it's not fixable, so there's no sense in discussing it."

"It must be about Carolyn St. John," Patty said, nodding decisively. "I may not have attended the family barbecue, but that doesn't mean I didn't hear that you brought a very lovely woman with you to meet the family."

"Whoa. You're putting the wrong emphasis on that. I brought Carolyn to the barbecue, and she met everyone there because the socially acceptable thing to do is introduce your date to those in attendance. You're making it sound as though Carolyn being with me was a big deal."

"The family thinks it was. Everyone really liked your Carolyn, by the way."

"She's not mine," Ryan said quietly. "I thought...well, I thought that Carolyn and I had something special together, but I was wrong. It turned out to be the same-old, same-old. The only reason I'm still…interacting with her…for the lack of a better word, is because I figured I could help smooth things a bit for Kimiko since I speak Korean. Carolyn and I are done, finished, kaput.''

"Why? What happened?''

Ryan turned his head to look at his sister with a frown. "Gosh, Patty, don't beat around the bush. Just speak right up and ask me what you want to know.''

"Well, excuse me,'' Patty said with an indignant little sniff. "A tad touchy, are we? This is tit for tat. You came to my house and demanded to know what was going on with me, why I had been practically invisible during the holidays, remember?''

"Because I love you, the whole family loves you, and it was apparent that things weren't as they should be with you. No joke. Man, I'd like to get my hands on that jerk Peter and…''

"We're not talking about me,'' Patty interrupted. "I will now quote the great Ryan Sharpe. I love you, the whole family loves you, and it's apparent that things aren't as they should be with you. What went wrong between you and Carolyn St. John?''

"Secrets, Patty,'' Ryan said, with a weary sigh. "Peter had his and they destroyed the world you two had created together. Carolyn had hers and…'' He shrugged.

"Are you in love with Carolyn St. John, Ryan?" Patty said.

"No. Well, hell, I don't think I am," he said, frowning.

"I've never been in love, so for all I know I could have missed the message, or the signals, or whatever, regarding how I feel about her. But that's a moot point, because what I had with Carolyn is over."

"And your heart hurts," Patty said quietly. "It actually physically aches because it's been smashed, shattered, and that's very painful."

"Yeah, it is," he said, his voice husky. "It really is."

"You wouldn't be experiencing that pain if you didn't love Carolyn. Trust me, I know. If I hadn't believed in my love for Peter and his for me with my entire heart and soul, what he has done wouldn't be causing me this terrible pain.

"I'd give anything to be blissfully happy with Peter the way we once were. Instead? I'm in the process of getting a divorce, will be a single mother of a two-year-old and will be giving birth to a baby fathered by a man who no longer loves me, nor is he the man I fell in love with. Nothing can change those facts."

"No, but I might change the shape of Peter's nose if I see him."

"My point is," Patty said, "my situation is etched in stone. Peter is gone, he's living with another woman, he no longer loves me, nor wants to be a part of my world.

"Oh, Ryan, are you certain you're not giving up on what you have with Carolyn too easily? So she had a secret, kept something from you. Can't you work through that, past it? Is her secret like Peter's? Is there someone else in her life?"

"No, it's nothing like that," he said, shaking his head. He paused and ran one hand over the back of his neck as he told Patty about Carolyn's revelation.

"Back up, here," Patty said, waving one hand in the air when he finished. "You broke things off with Carolyn. Not because she is hearing impaired but because she didn't tell you that she is. Do I have this straight?"

"Well…yeah," Ryan said. "There is no room for secrets in a relationship, Patty. You of all people ought to understand that. If there had really been something special between me and Carolyn, she would have shared her secret long before now."

"To match up with all your innermost secrets that you've shared with her, of course. You know, the difficulties you had because you felt different while you were growing up, a step off the mark, because you're half-Korean. You told her all of that because it's part of who you are as a person, a man, but she didn't reciprocate and tell you about her hearing problem. Do I still have this straight?''

Ryan opened his mouth to reply, then snapped it closed again.

"That's what I thought," Patty said, rolling her eyes heavenward. "And don't give me the spiel about your years of turmoil being personal, belonging only to you. I mean, my gosh, what could be more personal than being hearing impaired since you were a child and having to deal with everything it must have brought into that woman's life? You are so stubborn and dense sometimes, it's a crime. Men are such duds."

"Thanks a helluva lot," Ryan said, glaring at her.

"You're welcome," Patty snapped. "Darn it, Ryan, look at Kimiko. Look at that beautiful little boy. You could have a son like Kimiko, with your unique eyes and beautiful skin and light-up-a-room smile, if you would just listen to your heart for once in your life instead of the voices of your ghosts."

"I…"

"A dud," Patty said, getting to her feet. "Definitely a dud. Come on. You'd better take me and Tucker home so Kimiko won't be late for his tests at the hospital. What you ought to be thinking about, though, is if it's too *late* to fix things with the woman you're in love with, with Carolyn St. John.''

Chapter Twelve

Late that afternoon Carolyn and Ryan entered her apartment with Ryan carrying a sleeping Kimiko, and Carolyn toting the shopping bags containing his new clothes.

"He's really wiped out," Ryan said quietly. "Should I just put him to bed?"

"Yes, for now," Carolyn said, nodding as she set the bags on the floor. "We'll just take off his shoes so we don't wake him. I imagine he'll surface later and want something to eat."

When Kimiko was tucked into bed, the red baseball cap right next to him so he'd see it the moment he woke up, Carolyn and Ryan stood and watched him sleep.

"He was so brave," Carolyn whispered. "But that's really due to your easing his fears by talking to him, telling him everything would be fine. You were wonderful with him, Ryan."

"I'm glad I could help. He's sure a neat little kid, isn't he?"

"Yes. Yes, he is." Carolyn paused. "I wonder if there will be a way to keep in touch with him. I hate the idea of never seeing him again, not knowing how he's doing."

"I know what you mean. Maybe the program that sponsors these things has it set up so progress reports are sent back here."

"I'll definitely find out," she said, then sighed. "Oh, gracious, I'm as exhausted as Kimiko is. It's been a long, tense day. I think it was best, though, the way they did it, scheduling all the tests at once so he doesn't have to go through more tomorrow. They'll study the results, and the operation will be early the day after tomorrow. Oh, what a terrifying thought."

Ryan encircled Carolyn's shoulders with his arm. "He'll do fine. Matt told us that the surgeon is considered one of the best heart men in the country, remember?"

"I know. It's just that Kimiko is so small, so..."

Carolyn waved one hand in front of her face. "Don't get me started. I'm totally out of emotional energy about everything. If I dwell on any of the things on my mind right now, I'm going to go off on a crying jag. I really don't want to do that."

Kimiko stirred, then settled again.

"Let's leave him be before we wake him up," Carolyn said.

"Right."

But they didn't move. They just stood there, gazing at the sleeping child, Carolyn tucked closed to Ryan's side as he kept his arm around her shoulders.

Carolyn closed her eyes for a moment, savoring the warmth and strength of Ryan's body, allowing herself the luxury of feeling protected and cared for and not so alone, because she was so very, very tired. She leaned farther into him, resting her head on his chest, inhaling his aroma, something incredibly masculine that was simply him.

Ryan dipped his head and buried his face in Carolyn's silky, dark hair that smelled like flowers and sunshine. He raised his head again slowly, his hold on her tightening even more.

There they stood, he thought. The mother and father, watching their son sleeping peacefully after a hard day. They were in the midst of a crisis but would see it through together as a family united, gaining strength and courage from each other.

This was what he had always wanted.

This was what he'd told himself with a New Year's resolution he would no longer seek because it would never be his to have.

But now, right now, if he stepped away from reality, indulged in a flicker of fantasy it *was* his and, oh, God, it felt good—so right and real and his to cherish.

Patty's words suddenly slammed against Ryan's awareness and he stiffened, returning with a thud from where he'd mentally floated.

No, he thought fiercely. He had no intention of listening to whatever his heart might have to say in regard to his feelings for Carolyn St. John. It wouldn't matter what the message was, the truth, because the bottom line would remain the same.

"Yeah, well," Ryan said, dropping his arm from Carolyn's shoulders, "I'd better shove off. Maybe you can catch a nap before Kimiko wakes up and wants some dinner."

Carolyn blinked, then straightened. "What? Oh, yes, I think I will stretch out and at least relax for a while. I feel as though I've been climbing a mountain or something. I'll eat later with Kimiko."

They left the bedroom, both being extremely

careful not to brush against the other. In the living room Ryan went directly to the door, moving past the shopping bags.

"Thank you again for today," Carolyn said, stopping in the middle of the room. "For buying Kimiko so many nice things, for helping at the hospital. Thank you very much, Ryan."

"You're welcome," he said, one hand on the doorknob. "What's on the agenda for Kimiko tomorrow?"

"I'm taking the morning off, and we'll stay here to wait for the call from the hospital with the test results and instructions for his surgery. He can go to the office with me in the afternoon. If I break up his day between here and there, he hopefully won't get too bored."

Ryan nodded. "I have to drive up the coast tomorrow with a new client to look at his land and won't be back until late, but I'd like to be at the hospital when Kimiko has his surgery. Is that all right with you?"

"Yes, of course. Shall I call you with the time and— Yes, I'll call you."

"Fine. I'll have my answering machine on in case I'm not back yet when you call. Well, try to get some rest, Carolyn. I'll…I'll be waiting to hear from you with the details about the surgery schedule. So. See ya."

"See ya," she said softly.

"I..." Ryan started, then shook his head and yanked opened the door, closing it behind him with more force than was necessary as he left.

Carolyn cringed at the loud bang of the door, then went to the sofa and lay down, willing her mind blank, ordering herself not to cry, pleading with herself not to think. She was just going to sleep, sleep, sleep.

No, wait, she thought suddenly, swinging her feet to the floor. If she didn't unpack those shopping bags, Kimiko's new clothes would get wrinkled, and the last thing she wanted to do was iron.

As Carolyn removed the tags from Kimiko's outfits and folded each article neatly on a chair she found herself thinking about Patty, who had gone along on the shopping trip.

She hadn't even met Ryan's sister, Carolyn mused, but her heart just ached for Patty and the nightmare she was going through. She had so much to deal with she must feel completely overwhelmed, was probably finding it so difficult to see a light at the end of her dark tunnel.

Yet Patty had been willing to put her own troubles aside and go shopping with Ryan to see that Kimiko had the proper clothes to wear.

"I should call and thank her," Carolyn said, as she put the last little shirt on the pile of clothes.

"It's Patty…what? Patty, Patty…Clark. That's it. And Mr. Crummy's name is Peter."

Carolyn found the number for Peter Clark in the book, pressed the numbers on the telephone, then sank onto the end of the sofa as she heard the ringing on the other end of the line.

"Hello?"

"Patty? This is Carolyn St. John. You don't know me but…"

"I certainly know who you are, Carolyn," Patty interrupted, laughing. "The whole family knows who you are."

"Oh." Carolyn felt a flush stain her cheeks and cleared her throat. "I just wanted to call and thank you for helping Ryan shop for Kimiko. I just unpacked his new clothes and everything is so cute, just perfect. The red baseball cap is his favorite, of course."

"Ryan insisted that Kimiko have that cap. Then Ryan bent the bill of it just so, which always seems nuts to me. It's a guy thing, I guess. How did Kimiko's tests go this afternoon?"

"Fine. With Ryan there to communicate with Kimiko, everything went very smoothly. Ryan has been just wonderful through this business with Kimiko suddenly becoming my responsibility. I don't know what I would have done…would have done…without Ryan because… Oh, darn it, I'm getting all weepy. Ignore me. I'm just very tired. I just wanted to say thank you.''

"Carolyn, I'm an expert at becoming weepy these days. I assume Ryan told you what is happening in my life.''

"Well, yes, he did, and I'm so very sorry, Patty. My problems are nothing compared to what you're going through.''

"Your problems being in the form of my very stubborn brother. Right?''

"I...'' Carolyn laughed. "This conversation is getting all turned around. I should be attempting to comfort you in some way, and I feel as though I'm about to cry on your shoulder. You don't need this, me and my woes. You have enough on your plate.''

"Friends share, the good and the bad. I'd like to think that you and I might become friends. Wouldn't that be nice? A person can never have too many friends.'' She laughed again. "We can go to lunch sometime and tell each other to keep our chins up and all that good rot. Then we'll cry together until we're soggy.''

"You've got a date.'' Carolyn laughed. "They'll probably throw us out of the restaurant for wailing our little hearts out.''

"Carolyn,'' Patty said, her voice serious, "listen to me. Okay? My life with Peter, my world as I've known it, is over. I have no choice but to accept that…somehow…and attempt to move forward. But I need to say this to you. Don't give up on Ryan and what you have together.''

''I—''

''It may seem hopeless right now,'' Patty went on, ''but give it some time. Ryan is a wonderful man, but he's also very—oh, what word do I want?—complex, with layers beneath the surface. But, Carolyn? Ryan cares for you very much. I know he does. He just needs to sift and sort through the mess he's made of his male mind. Men can be very slow at figuring things out.''

''I—''

''No, don't comment now on what I said. Just think about it. I'm so pleased that you called, and I'm looking forward to meeting you in person. New friends. Isn't that a lovely thought?''

''Yes. Yes, it is,'' Carolyn said. ''We'll get together very soon. And thank you again for helping with the shopping spree.''

''It was my pleasure. It's always fun to spend someone else's money. That Kimiko is a doll. I just wanted to hug him to pieces.''

''He's a special little boy,'' Carolyn said softly. ''Goodbye, Patty. It was wonderful talking with you.''

''''Bye for now.''

Carolyn replaced the receiver, then stared at it.

Patty Clark was a very remarkable woman, she thought. Despite the painful shambles her life had become, she had reached beyond herself, voiced concern that Carolyn would give up on complex, stubborn Ryan, on what they had together.

Oh, wouldn't it be fantastic if Patty was right? Carolyn thought, stretching out on the sofa again. Ryan just needed time to straighten out his head or some such thing, then would come charging in on his mighty white horse and carry her off into the sunset to live with him, happily ever after.

Well, Patty, her new friend Patty, was sadly wrong about any future that Carolyn St. John might have with Ryan Sharpe. It was over, what they had shared, just as it was with Patty and Peter. Over.

Many hours later Ryan muttered an earthy expletive, snapped on the lamp next to his bed and flung back the blankets to sit up on the edge of the bed. He propped his elbows on his knees, dragged his hands down his face, then scowled at the clock on the nightstand.

Two-thirty in the morning, he fumed, and he hadn't slept a wink. He was so tired he was punchy, but all he'd done was toss and turn and chase a jumble of thoughts around in his mind in a maddening circle. And there, always there, were Patty's haunting words.

Ryan sighed, then straightened and rotated his neck in an attempt to loosen the tense muscles that were producing a throbbing headache. As he swung his head around, his glance fell on the globe where it sat on top of the dresser, and his heart quickened. He got to his feet and retrieved the delicate gift, cradling it in both hands. Hands, he realized that were trembling slightly as he sat back down on the side of the bed.

He stared at the exquisite globe and relived once again the meeting with Robert MacAllister, remembering all that had been said in his grandfather's study.

"Be at peace with who I am," Ryan said quietly, "even though I'm different. Like...like Carolyn has done despite the fact that *she* is different."

Yes, Ryan thought, his mind racing. Carolyn could have used her hearing impairment as an excuse to withdraw from the world, live at home with her parents, not run the risk of being rejected if she stepped forward.

But not Carolyn St. John. She'd gone after her dreams and achieved her goals. No one at the adoption agency even knew she wore hearing aids, because Carolyn wanted to be, and was, accepted for who she was as a woman and a highly respected professional in her chosen field. Yes, Carolyn was different from the norm, but it didn't matter one iota. Nor did she judge others by their differences. She believed in her work, in the rightness of creating loving families by the addition of a child from another country. That child wouldn't look like his adoptive parents, but would it matter? No, oh, no, because love was stronger, more powerful, than the stumbling blocks of prejudice the family might encounter as the years went by.

When Carolyn St. John looked at him, Ryan Sharpe, did she immediately make a mental list of how different he was from other men she had dated? No. She saw him, judged him, had accepted him and shared the most intimate act there was between two people with him—the man, the person.

Did Carolyn catalog Kimiko as a cute little Korean boy every time she looked at him? No. To her Kimiko was a beautiful, heart-stealing child, who just happened to be Korean.

"My God," Ryan said, his gaze riveted on the globe. "What have I done?"

He hadn't trusted and believed in *her* enough to share his innermost secrets with her. *He* had rejected *her,* had declared her guilty of prejudices she didn't possess. And when she'd bared her soul, he'd turned his back and walked away from her without a word spoken. He'd left her believing that, because she was different, what they'd had together was over.

"Oh, Carolyn," Ryan said, his voice choked with emotion, "I'm so sorry. I've hurt you so much because all I could think about was myself, my selfish, self-centered self. I'm just so...damn... sorry."

Ryan lifted the globe to eye level and stared at it with tear-filled eyes.

"This is my world," he said. "All of it. I'm half-American and half-Korean and together they make me whole, complete, who I am. This is my world and I want to share it with you, Carolyn St. John, because... Oh, God, Carolyn, I love you so much, with all that I am."

Chapter Thirteen

At ten o'clock in the morning on the day of Kimiko's surgery, Carolyn stood next to the hospital bed and sifted her fingers through Kimiko's silky hair.

"Ry?" Kimiko said, as he hugged his baseball cap to his tiny chest.

"Ry will be here, Kimiko. I left him a message on his answering machine yesterday, remember? Don't get upset, sweetheart. Oh, Kimiko, I wish you could understand me. Everything is going to be fine, you'll see. I know you're scared but..."

"Ry!" Kimiko said, attempting to sit up.

"Whoa," Ryan said, striding into the room. "What's all this fussing about?"

"Ry," Kimiko said, smiling as he settled back onto the pillow.

"I'm sorry I'm late," Ryan said, looking at Carolyn. "There was an accident on the freeway and traffic was backed up and..."

There she was, he thought. The woman he loved. There was Carolyn.

"Well, you're here now. Kimiko was getting all in a dither because he wanted to see you. It's so frustrating for me to not be able to communicate with him, ease his fears. I envy you your ability to speak Korean, Ryan."

"I've become rather pleased about it myself," he said, then switched his gaze to Kimiko and spoke to him in the language they both understood.

Kimiko listened to Ryan intently, frowned, then shook his head. Ryan continued to talk, then slowly, very slowly, Kimiko extended the treasured baseball cap toward Ryan, who took it in both hands, then bowed slightly.

"Thank goodness," Carolyn said. "He wouldn't let me have it and I thought they'd have to take it from him once he was asleep. I was worried about his reaction when he woke up later and it wasn't there."

"He's trusting me to keep it safe for him. This

kiddo just keeps giving and giving, doesn't he? He makes me feel about ten feet tall.''

''Is this the show we're getting on the road?'' a man said, coming into the room. ''Hey, Kimiko, I'm the guy who is going to fix that little ticker of yours.''

Ryan spoke to Kimiko in Korean and he nodded.

''Okay, folks,'' the doctor said. ''Hit the waiting room and drink some of our lousy coffee. This little munchkin will be as good as new in a couple of hours.'' He turned as another man came into the room. ''We're ready to roll here, Jerry.''

''Oh, but...'' Carolyn said.

''Give Kimiko a kiss, Carolyn,'' Ryan said.

''Yes. Okay. I'm a wreck.'' She leaned over the side rail on the bed and kissed Kimiko on the forehead. ''See you soon, baby boy.''

Kimiko said something to Ryan, who nodded and wiggled the baseball cap, then Ryan kissed him on the cheek. Jerry pushed the bed out of the room, the surgeon patted Carolyn on the shoulder, then Ryan took her elbow and led her to a waiting room down the hall.

''I'm hating this,'' Carolyn said, sinking onto a vinyl sofa. ''I am really, really hating this, Ryan.''

Ryan sat down next to her, then placed the baseball cap carefully on the coffee table in front of the couch.

"Look at that hat," he said.

"What?"

"Look at Kimiko's baseball cap, Carolyn."

"Okay, I am."

"Do you realize that he's never been able to chase a baseball, swing a bat, run the bases, because he just didn't have the energy? Once his heart is fixed, he'll be a normal little boy who can play ball with that cap worn with pride. That's really something, isn't it?"

They turned their heads at the same moment and their gazes met.

"Yes," Carolyn said, nodding. "It is. There are so many wonderful adventures waiting for him that he's never had the chance to explore."

"Sometimes we need a tangible object to focus on to center us, get us thinking straight."

"Like Kimiko's baseball cap."

Ryan nodded. And like a beautiful, antique globe given in love by a man who possessed such wisdom it defied description.

"Later today, after we know Kimiko is all right, have seen him, then left here, I'd like the chance to talk to you if you're willing to listen to me, Carolyn. Please?"

"I don't think…"

"Please, Carolyn?"

Carolyn got to her feet and began to pace around the small room.

Talk about what? she thought. What more was there to say? Nothing. Oh, she had a newsflash she could toss in the ring, a real wing-ding of a heart-breaking report. Somewhere in the middle of her nearly sleepless night she'd run out of places to hide from the truth.

She was in love with Ryan Sharpe.

It was the dumbest, dopiest thing she'd ever done in her entire life, but there it was. She'd fallen in love with Ryan. But *that* ditzy data was definitely not going to be part of whatever it was that Ryan wished to discuss with her. No, no, no.

"Carolyn?"

She stopped her trek and sighed. "All right, Ryan, we'll talk later, after we know that everything is fine with Kimiko. But I really don't see that there's anything left to say."

"There's a great deal to say." He paused. "Well, we'd better settle in here and get comfortable because we're in for a wait that is probably going to seem about ten days long."

Carolyn sank back onto the sofa. "I'm really, really hating this."

Ryan chuckled. "That has been duly noted, Ms. St. John. Want some coffee?"

"No, thank you. I'll just sit here and count the tile squares in the floor, or something."

"Whatever works."

A heavy silence fell over the room as neither of them spoke for the next fifteen minutes, each lost in their own thoughts.

And then they came.

The MacAllisters.

Matt entered the room, saying he'd snuck away from a desk covered in paperwork upstairs, but he wanted to be where he'd hear the very first report on how Kimiko's surgery had gone.

Margaret and Robert were next, carrying a colorful balloon bouquet, followed five minutes later by Patty, who produced a teddy bear in a baseball uniform, complete with a cap just like Kimiko's. Carolyn and Patty shared a hug.

Jessica came, and Emily and Mark, then Forrest and Jillian, Bobby and Diane, Ted and Hannah, and on and on, until the room could hold no more people and the overflow talked quietly out in the hallway.

Carolyn realized from the snatches of conversation she heard that they hadn't planned this show of support together, but that each had come on their own with a specially chosen gift for Kimiko, knowing it was where they wanted to be. And yet none of them were surprised in the least to see the others.

Dear heaven, she thought, she was going to burst into tears. What an incredibly wonderful, loving family this was, a family she would be a part of if Ryan loved her as she did him.

Oh, Carolyn, don't, she admonished herself. Loving a man who didn't love her was torture enough without dwelling on these remarkable people she'd probably never see again after today. When she got on with her life. Alone. So very, very alone—and lonely.

There were so many conversations taking place that time passed quickly and Carolyn's heart skipped a beat when she saw the surgeon cutting a path through the throng of MacAllisters. Silence fell and all eyes were riveted on the doctor.

"Kimiko sure has a big fan club," the doctor said. "Well, ladies and gentlemen, I'm happy to announce that Kimiko Sung came through the surgery with flying colors, his heart is repaired, and I have a feeling that baseball cap there on the table is going to get a real workout when that little fella gets back to Korea ready to play ball."

"Oh, thank God," Carolyn whispered, pressing her trembling fingertips against her lips.

"Kimiko is in recovery. He came around enough to satisfy me, but he's zonked again, which is fine," the doctor went on. "No visitors until this evening, and if you come then, keep it short and sweet, in and out. If all goes well, he'll be ready to return to Korea in about three days. I'll give you my final word on that later. Okay? Are we cool? I'm ready for lunch…big time."

"Wait," Ryan said, snatching up the baseball cap from the table. "Would you tuck this next to Kimiko so he'll see it when he's fully awake? It's very important to him. I promised him I'd keep it safe until he could have it back after the surgery."

"Sure thing," the doctor said, taking the red cap. "A promise made should be a promise kept. Hey, Matt, is this a family reunion of yours? Are we charging you rent for the space you guys are taking up?" He waved at the group and left the room.

Excited chatter exploded in the room over the wonderful news about Kimiko, and hugs were exchanged.

"I don't know whether to laugh or cry, Ryan," Carolyn said. "I'm so grateful that— No, I'm shutting up. I'm definitely going to cry."

"There aren't too many dry eyes in this room," Ryan said, glancing around.

"I can't believe how your family suddenly appeared here. They didn't plan it, they just all did it. They're wonderful people."

"Yes, they are," Ryan said, his gaze meeting Robert's across the room. Ryan nodded slightly, and Robert smiled, a very serene, satisfied smile. "They really are."

Matt was loaded up with gifts with the promise he would see that they got to the room where Kimiko would be taken once he was out of recovery. The group dispersed, wandering down the hallway with Jessica and Emily announcing they were going to take a detour and go peek at the babies in the maternity wing.

"Well, we're back where we started," Ryan said finally. "Just the two of us." He paused. "Look, we need some lunch. Why don't you go on home, I'll pick up some hamburgers and meet you at your place. It's time for that talk we're going to have. Okay?"

"Maybe we should postpone whatever it is you wish to discuss, Ryan," Carolyn said, not quite meeting his gaze. "I mean, this has been an emotionally draining series of hours and it might be best to wait."

"No, Carolyn, it can't wait. In fact, it's long overdue."

"Could you give me a teeny little hint as to what this is about?"

"The world, two worlds," Ryan said. "A globe that held the answers I finally understood. Go on home, Carolyn, and I'll be there soon. Soon. I just hope and pray that I'm not too late.''

By the time Ryan arrived at Carolyn's apartment with the promised hamburgers, she was a nervous wreck from wondering what on earth Ryan wished to discuss with her. She could not for the life of her think of anything they had left to say to each other. What they had shared was over.

Carolyn sank onto a chair at the table as Ryan distributed the food, telling herself that she had to eat before she fainted dead out on her face. She'd been too stressed about Kimiko to have breakfast, but now didn't see how she could possibly swallow one bite of lunch.

''Eat,'' she said, picking up the hamburger and taking a bite.

''Want some blood?'' Ryan said, holding up a little packet.

Carolyn smiled in spite of herself and snatched the ketchup packet from Ryan's hand.

''It seems hard to believe that Kimiko will be able to go home so soon after heart surgery, doesn't it?'' Ryan said, then ate a few French fries.

''Yes, it does,'' Carolyn said. ''But I did some research on the Internet yesterday afternoon at the office, and everything I found said that once that hole in the heart is repaired the patient's recovery is very fast and the changes in their overall physical condition are remarkable.''

She paused. ''I think I'd better buy Kimiko another suitcase so he can get all his lovely gifts from your family home to Korea. Oh, this is ridiculous, Ryan. I'm not going to sit here chomping on a hamburger I don't even want and chitchat with you with this mysterious cloud hanging over us. What do you want to discuss with me?''

This was it, Ryan thought. What he said in the next few minutes and how Carolyn received it would determine his future happiness. Yes, this was it. He was listening to his heart at long last.

Ryan swallowed the last bite of his hamburger, took a deep breath and let it out slowly.

''Okay, here goes. First of all, Carolyn, there has been a terrible misunderstanding, and it's all my fault. When you told me about your hearing problem, the fact that you wear hearing aids, I got up and left this apartment without saying one word to you.''

''I'm very aware of that,'' she said, dunking another fry in a puddle of ketchup. ''I really don't want to relive that scenario, Ryan.''

''We have to,'' he said, a tad too loudly. ''Sorry. I didn't mean to yell. Carolyn, I know how you must have perceived what I did. You thought I was rejecting you because you had a physical impairment. That isn't true, I swear it isn't. I am, in fact, so proud of you, am in awe of what you've accomplished, how you set your goals and didn't rest until you got where you wanted to go, despite the fact that you have a hearing problem.''

Carolyn looked up at him and frowned. ''That's not the impression you gave when I told you about it, Ryan. Not even close.''

''I know and I'm so damn sorry. My reaction was selfish and self-centered. I turned what you were telling me inward, did a real poor-me number about how you didn't trust and believe in me enough to tell me the truth until I pushed you to the point that you didn't have any choice. I saw your silence as a rejection of *me*.''

''Oh, but that's not...''

''I know, I know,'' he interrupted. ''I've finally got my head on straight. After all these years and all that pain. Remember how I said I didn't enjoy my trip to Korea when I went?''

''Yes.''

''That's because I went with a chip on my shoulder. I didn't have an open mind or heart. I was immediately looking for all the ways I didn't fit in there, either, all the ways I was different. And I found them, sure I did.

''Now, thanks to a special gift from my grandfather, a verbal pop in the chops from my sister, a little boy named Kimiko Sung and to you, Carolyn St. John, my battle is over. I've won. I'm Ryan Sharpe. I'm half-American and half-Korean, and I'm at peace with that at long last.''

''Well, that's great,'' Carolyn said. She was so happy for him. Ryan had fought his demons and won the war and now had his whole life ahead of him to live, to laugh…to love. If only…no. ''Really great.''

''There's something else I want to say to you, Carolyn,'' Ryan said, covering one of her hands with one of his on top of the table. ''Carolyn, I love you. I love you so much. I want to spend the rest of my life with you, have children, little miracles with you. Children who will be different in a way, but God knows they'll be loved. I am deeply in love with you, Carolyn St. John.''

Carolyn's heart began to beat with such a rapid tempo she could hear the echo of it drumming in her ears. She opened her mouth to speak, shook her head slightly and snapped her mouth closed again as she stared at Ryan with wide eyes.

''Carolyn,'' Ryan said his voice ringing with emotion as he tightened his hold on her hand. ''Do *you* love *me?* Would you do me the honor of marrying me? Please?''

Carolyn pulled her hand free as unwanted tears filled her eyes. ''No, I won't marry you, Ryan.''

No, Ryan's mind screamed. Don't say that, Carolyn, please don't say that.

"Well," he said, his voice unsteady, "I'll just go and leave you alone and… Whew. Talk about making a fool of myself, huh? I thought you felt the same way about me that I do about you and…"

"I won't marry you," Carolyn said, attempting to blink away her tears, "despite the fact that I love you with every breath in my body and I daydream about holding our baby in my arms. No, I won't marry you because you still have secrets that you refuse to share with me, secrets that have the power to destroy us."

"You love me?"

Carolyn nodded, tears choking off any further words she might have spoken.

Ryan got to his feet and came around the table. "Let's go into the living room. It's time I shared my secrets with you, because you're right, they're very powerful, could destroy us, and I don't intend to allow that to happen. I've never told anyone what I'm about to divulge to you." He extended one hand toward her.

Carolyn hesitated, then placed her hand in Ryan's, allowing him to draw her to her feet and lead her into the living room. She sank onto the sofa and watched as he settled in the easy chair.

He rested his elbows on his knees and clasped his hands.

"Carolyn," he said, "did you go to your senior prom in high school?"

"Pardon me?" she said, obviously confused.

"Did you? Go to the prom?"

"No," she said. "No one asked me. I was so shy and withdrawn. On the night of the prom my parents tried to make it up to me by taking me out to dinner at a fancy restaurant. That was a disaster because there were a dozen prom couples eating there before the dance.

"It was a horrible night, emphasized how different I was. I felt so rejected and lonely. I haven't thought about prom night in years. Why are we talking about this?"

"Right there, what you just said shows how much stronger you are than I am. You managed to put away the painful memories of your prom night and moved forward with your life. Me? I got emotionally mired in what happened to me on the big event of the prom, and it affected me from that night forward."

"I don't understand," Carolyn said, looking at him intently.

"I was really struggling at that age with being different. Teen years are tough enough but I was on overload. I gathered my courage and asked a girl to the senior prom. Man, my folks were so thrilled that I had taken that step. They bought me a tuxedo, then rented a limo for the evening so I could escort my date to the dance in style.

"When I arrived at her house with an orchid in a plastic box topped by a pink bow, her father answered the door. The man roared in anger when he saw me. He screamed at me, said no daughter of his was going anywhere with a slanty-eyed foreigner, then slammed the door in my face."

"Oh, dear God," Carolyn whispered, as fresh tears filled her eyes.

"I...I told the limo driver to leave," Ryan went on, getting to his feet, "then I tossed the corsage in the gutter and walked. I walked for hours and hours, then finally went home. I told my parents that I'd had a super time at the dance and that my date had been the prettiest girl there. I didn't have the courage to tell my mother and father that their son had been rejected, turned away at the door."

"Oh, Ryan, I'm so sorry," Carolyn said, nearly choking on a sob.

"I never really moved past that horrifying experience, Carolyn. I didn't deal with it properly. I just settled in with the attitude that the rejection would come, at some point through the remainder of my life, it would always come. And, of course, it did, because I was watching, waiting, making mountains out of what were probably not even molehills. I also made certain that I dated women who were more totally centered on their careers, weren't even considering being part of a serious relationship.''

"To protect yourself," Carolyn said, her voice trembling. "You built walls to fend off the rejection before it could reach you, hurt you. Rejection that might not even have come."

"Yes. But then I met you, and from the very first moment there was something special between us, rare and wonderful, and like nothing I'd experienced before. I allowed myself to fantasize that maybe, just maybe, things would be different this time. Then I'd pull back, get tough, tell myself to quit chasing windmills. But my heart was speaking louder than my ghosts, and I was slowly but surely falling in love with you.

"Then you told me about your hearing aids and... Ah, Carolyn, I blew it so badly...flung back in time, felt like that pathetic kid on the front porch holding an orchid in a plastic box with a pink bow on top, and just like on the night of the prom I walked away without saying a word.

"There's no excuse for what I did to you that night, Carolyn, but I'm asking you to forgive me. I'm so sorry, just so damn sorry. I love you, will always love you. I want to spend the rest of my life with you, but if I've hurt you so badly that you can't forgive me, then…''

Carolyn got to her feet, ran across the room and flung herself into Ryan's arms, causing him to stagger from the impact. He wrapped his arms around her as she encircled his neck with her hands.

"I love you, Ryan Sharpe," she said, tears spilling onto her cheeks. "Yes, I'll forgive you, because I understand now what really happened. I understand because there are no more secrets between us."

"Will you marry me?" Ryan said, his voice husky with emotion.

"Oh, yes, I will marry you, stand by your side as your partner in life. You are my soul mate, Ryan."

"Ah, Carolyn," Ryan said, then captured her lips with his in a searing kiss.

Carolyn returned the kiss in total abandon, giving of herself completely.

It was a kiss of forgiveness, of understanding and of a commitment to the future—together. The kiss held the power to fling into oblivion past pain and tears shed. It was a kiss of promise, hope, love and the greatest joy they had ever known.

Ryan ended the kiss slowly, reluctantly, then spoke close to Carolyn's lips.

"I want you. I want to make love with you, Carolyn. I want to make love with the woman I love with all my heart, my mind, my very soul."

"Yes. I want you, too. This is such a special day."

"Oh, indeed it is. It's the first day of the rest of our lives together."

They went down the hall to the bedroom, where sunlight poured over the bed like a glorious golden waterfall. An urgency suffused them, their desire bursting into licking flames of heat within them. They shed their clothes, swept back the blankets, then tumbled onto the bed, reaching immediately for the other, the moments of separation far too long.

"The magic," Carolyn whispered, gazing into Ryan's dark, mesmerizing eyes. "It's here again, just like before. Can you feel it, Ryan? The magic?"

"Oh, yes, my darling Carolyn. I can feel it. It will always be here for us, because we create it when we're together. It's ours forever."

"I love you, Ryan."

His lips melted over hers, and tongues met in the sweet darkness of her mouth, dueling, dancing, stroking, as hands roamed with gentle caresses, leaving heated paths as they went.

The tension built within them, but they held

back, anticipating what would come, savoring the taste, the aroma, the very essence of the other.

"My life," Ryan murmured. "My wife."

"My husband," Carolyn whispered. "And the father of the children I pray we'll be blessed with. A whole houseful of little Kimikos."

Ryan chuckled. "I think I'd better start over on those plans I'm drawing for the house and add a few more bedrooms. We'll design our home together, Carolyn, make it perfect for us and our children. It will be filled with love and laughter."

"With no space for secrets."

"No. No secrets. Never again." Ryan swept his heated gaze over Carolyn's body. "You are so beautiful."

Then no more words were spoken as they gave way to their passion. When they became one, the magic seemed to grow in its intensity, meshing them into a single entity that joined not just their bodies but their hearts, their minds, their souls as well.

They moved as one. The tempo was wild and wonderful, carrying them up and away to the summit of the sunshine waterfall, then over the top to be flung to their private place.

"Ryan, oh, Ryan!"

"I love you, Carolyn."

They clung tightly to each other as though

they'd never again let go, savoring every ecstasy-filled sensation as wave after wave of release swept through them, then quieted into gentle ripples as they floated back down to the golden pool of sunlight on the bed.

Then nestled close they slept, dreaming the dreams of all the tomorrows they would share together.

Carolyn stirred, opened her eyes, then a soft smile formed on her lips as she looked at Ryan who was sleeping peacefully beside her.

Oh, how she loved him, she thought. They had weathered such difficult storms together and now the future was theirs to have and to hold, to love and to cherish, from this day forward.

How strange it was, she mused. A little boy named Kimiko Sung had come from halfway around the world because he needed help, needed his heart healed.

"And a child shall lead them," Carolyn whispered.

It was because of Kimiko, really, that she and Ryan had been kept together when they were hurt and angry, prepared to end things, go their separate ways. It hadn't been just Kimiko's heart that had been healed but hers and Ryan's, as well.

Carolyn stiffened suddenly, glanced at the clock, then sat bolt upright on the bed.

"Kimiko," she said, then reached over and wiggled Ryan's shoulder. "Ryan, wake up. We've got to shower and dress, eat something and get to the hospital to see Kimiko. We can't let him think we forgot about him. Ryan."

"Mmm," Ryan said, not opening his eyes.

"Ryan. Think about Kimiko. That poor baby is probably sitting in the bed staring at the door to his room and wondering where we are. Maybe he's crying. Maybe he's... Wake up."

Ryan's eyes shot open. "I'm awake. No, I'm not. Yes, I am. Cripes, it's nearly dark in here. We've got to get to the hospital and see Kimiko."

"Gosh," Carolyn said, laughing, "I'm glad you thought of that."

"Hurry. Oh, man, if he's upset I'll feel like a bum." Ryan slid off the bed. "Do you think he's crying?"

Kimiko was definitely *not* crying.

He was propped against the pillows on the bed, his trusty red baseball cap on his head, devoting his full attention to a hand-held electronic game he was playing with. The other gifts he'd received from the MacAllisters were spread across the foot of the bed.

"Hi, Kimiko," Ryan said, coming to the side of the bed with Carolyn.

Kimiko nodded, his little fingers busily pushing buttons on the toy.

"I don't think he missed us," Carolyn said, smiling. "Oh, Ryan, can you believe how fantastic he looks. It's hard to believe he had heart surgery this morning."

Ryan encircled Carolyn's shoulders with his arm and tucked her close to his side.

"A lot of miraculous things have happened since this morning, my future wife."

"That's very true, my future husband."

Kimiko glanced up and smiled. "Ry. Caro. Hi. Hi."

"Hi," they said in unison.

The doctor entered the room and came to the foot of the bed.

"Okay, folks, that's it for tonight. This munchkin is ready for dreamland."

"But we just got here," Ryan said.

"You can see him tomorrow," the doctor said.

"He looks super," Carolyn said.

"He came through with flying colors. We'll monitor him for a couple of days, fill him up with nourishing food, then send him home to Korea to his mom and dad. We're in the process of getting a message to his folks now that all is well. Before long they'll all forget that there was a time that Kimiko's heart was…well, broken.''

Carolyn and Ryan exchanged a loving smile.

"Yes," Carolyn said. "We'll all be able to forget about broken hearts.''

Three days later Carolyn sniffled into a hankie as the airplane carrying Kimiko disappeared into the heavens.

"Oh-h-h," she said. "Ryan, how can I be so happy and so sad at the same time? I'm so grateful that Kimiko is a healthy, happy little boy, and he was so eager to see his parents again. But he became such an important part of our lives so quickly, and I'm going to miss him. He gave me such a sweet hug goodbye and… Oh-h-h.''

Ryan chuckled, then dropped a kiss on the top of Carolyn's head.

"We knew this parting would be tough, but to take your mind off Kimiko leaving I've planned a special evening for us.''

"Really?" Carolyn said, then dabbed at her nose again with the hanky. "What are we going to do tonight?''

"It's a surprise. I'll pick you up at seven o'clock sharp. Wear the fanciest dress you own. We're going to do it up to the nines.''

* * *

A tingle of excitement swept through Carolyn as she nodded in approval at her reflection in the mirror in her bedroom.

This dress, she thought, smiling, was a tad more daring than anything she'd worn before. But when she'd made a dash to the stores after work it had been in the window of a boutique and seemed to be calling her name.

"Aren't you just sexy as all get-out," she said, turning one way, then the other.

The slim skirt fell to her knees, but it was the camisole top that had caught her attention. It had minuscule straps and tiny vertical rows of delicate lace. The material draped to the top of her breasts, giving a tantalizing peek of what was beneath. The color was gorgeous, a sea green with a pearly tone that shimmered as the light caught it from different directions.

Strappy evening sandals, she mentally cataloged, a lacy shawl and a small purse. Freshly shampooed hair, just the right touch of makeup and floral cologne dabbed on her wrists and the base of her throat.

A knock at the door sent her hurrying down the hall and across the living room to fling open the door. Ryan entered the apartment, then turned to face Carolyn as she closed the door.

Her gaze swept over him, her eyes widening as she scrutinized every magnificent inch of him.

He was wearing a perfectly tailored tuxedo, crisp white shirt with tucks and gold studs and a satin cummerbund.

And in his hand was a clear plastic box containing a beautiful orchid. On top of the box was a pink satin bow.

"You look sensational, Carolyn. We'd better go. I have a limo waiting downstairs. We're going to have our very own prom tonight. We'll put to rest the last of the painful past, so we'll be totally and absolutely free to move forward together."

"Oh, Ryan," Carolyn said, feeling as though her heart was actually going to burst with love for Ryan Sharpe, "this is the sweetest, most romantic…" She smiled. "We're going to the prom."

"Yes, we are, and after we've danced the night away," Ryan said, love shining in his dark eyes, "we'll begin the journey toward our forever. I love you, Carolyn."

"And I love you, Ryan. I'm ready to go, my darling. I'm very, very ready to go."

Epilogue

The six-seat airplane popped out of a fluffy cloud to give a tantalizing glimpse of the land below, then was once again gobbled up by another cloud. The hum of the engines, plus a very generous dose of jet lag lulled Carolyn into a rather dreamy state.

She glanced at Ryan, who was sitting next to her, scrutinizing a map with deep concentration.

Ryan Sharpe, Carolyn thought, a soft smile forming on her lips. Her husband. Her soul mate. Her partner for life. Dear heaven, how she loved him.

She leaned her head back on the top of the seat

and closed her eyes, deciding to indulge in a lovely trip down memory lane by remembering the last four months.

Their wedding in early February in a quaint little church in Ventura had been perfect. Her parents had flown in for the ceremony, all the MacAllisters had been there, as well as Carolyn's friends from the adoption agency. She'd worn a white, street-length dress that had been lovely in its simplicity and carried a bouquet of baby orchids to represent the glorious night that Ryan had created their very own prom.

They'd honeymooned in San Francisco where their little miracle was conceived, then returned to move Carolyn's belongings into Ryan's apartment, which was much larger than hers. Over the following weeks they'd worked diligently on the plans Ryan was drawing up for their house that would become a home from the moment they moved into it.

Then Ryan had approached her about making this trip, and she'd been thrilled. So, here they were hopping from one marshmallow cloud to another in this teeny-tiny plane.

The sounds of the engines changed, and Carolyn lifted her head and looked out the window. The plane was beginning its descent to a narrow landing strip she could see below. There was also a small building that was the only structure as far as the eye could see.

"How are you doing, sweetheart?" Ryan asked Carolyn, as he finished folding the map. "This puddle-jumper didn't exactly provide a smooth ride from the main airport. Are you and your passenger all right?"

Carolyn smiled and patted her slightly rounded stomach. "We're just fine. He's fluttering around in there, doing an impression of this funny little airplane, I think, but all is well."

"She. I keep telling you, Carolyn," Ryan said. "We're having a girl."

"Nope," Carolyn said. "I'm going to go over this with you one more time, Ryan. Maggie had a boy, then Emily had a girl, followed by Jessica's boy, then very quickly after that was Alice's girl. It's very simple, my sweet, the next baby born will be a boy."

"And I keep reminding you that Patty's baby is due before ours. What if *she* has the boy?"

Carolyn laughed. "Then my great theory will be shot and baby Sharpe will be a girl, which will make you obnoxiously right."

Ryan dropped a quick kiss on Carolyn's lips. "Yep. By the way, Mrs. Sharpe, I love you."

"And I love... Oh! We're landing."

The plane bumped onto the runway, slowed, then came to a shuddering stop. The door opened and a set of stairs was lowered to the tarmac. Ryan preceded Carolyn out the door to stand at the top of the stairs, then extended his hand to her to bring her to his side.

"Welcome to Korea," he said. "Welcome to my other home. I'm just as proud to be a part of this one as I am of the one we left on the other side of the world. There's so much I want to show you during the two weeks we'll be visiting here. This is part of my heritage."

"And part of our baby's heritage, too," Carolyn said, smiling at him warmly.

They made their way down the steps and started toward the small building. The door was flung open, and a man and woman came out, waving to them in the distance.

And then there he was…Kimiko.

He dashed around his parents and ran full speed toward Carolyn and Ryan, his red baseball cap firmly on his head. In a blur of healthy-little-boy energy, he ran to greet his special friends, so excited to see them again, eager to welcome them… home.

* * * * *

Be sure to watch for Matt's story coming to Silhouette Special Edition in 2004.

SILHOUETTE®
SPECIAL EDITION™

AVAILABLE FROM 21ST NOVEMBER 2003

RYAN'S PLACE Sherryl Woods

The Devaneys

Ryan Devaney didn't believe in love—until he met Maggie O'Brien. Her bright smile and tender touch warmed his frozen spirit and awakened forgotten desires—but dare Ryan dream of a happily-ever-after?

SCROOGE AND THE SINGLE GIRL
Christine Rimmer

The Sons of Caitlin Bravo

All Will Bravo wanted for the festive season was to be left alone. Then in walked beautiful Jilly Diamond, who tempted him beyond all reason. Suddenly Jilly was *everything* Will desired for Christmas.

THEIR INSTANT BABY Cathy Gillen Thacker

The Deveraux Legacy

When Amy Deveraux agreed to babysit her godson she hadn't known she'd be sharing her duties with sexy Nick Everton. But seeing Nick with the baby made Amy yearn for something *much* more permanent.

THE COWBOY'S CHRISTMAS MIRACLE
Anne McAllister

Code of the West

Single mum Erin Jones had never expected to see her unrequited crush Deke Malone again—especially not with a two-year-old son! His maleness set Erin on fire—but would they get a second chance at love?

RACE TO THE ALTAR Patricia Hagan

Under different circumstances racing driver Rick Castles would've stopped at nothing to make Liz Mallory his. But his career hurt relationships. *Could* he risk the ultimate race with Liz—to the altar?

HER SECRET AFFAIR Arlene James

A business contract was all Chey and millionaire Brodie Todd were supposed to have. Except they couldn't stop their overwhelming attraction. But could Chey risk her heart on this powerful, handsome single father?

**SILHOUETTE®
SPECIAL EDITION™**

proudly presents

a brand-new five-book series from
bestselling author

SHERRYL WOODS

The Devaneys

*Five brothers torn apart in childhood,
reunited by love.*

RYAN'S PLACE
December 2003

SEAN'S RECKONING
January 2004

MICHAEL'S DISCOVERY
February 2004

PATRICK'S DESTINY
March 2004

DANIEL'S DESIRE
April 2004

1203/SH/LC75

FREE!

4 Books
and a surprise gift!

We would like to take this opportunity to thank you for reading this Silhouette® book by offering you the chance to take FOUR more specially selected titles from the Special Edition™ series absolutely FREE! We're also making this offer to introduce you to the benefits of the Reader Service™—

- ★ FREE home delivery
- ★ FREE gifts and competitions
- ★ FREE monthly Newsletter
- ★ Books available before they're in the shops
- ★ Exclusive Reader Service discount

Accepting these FREE books and gift places you under no obligation to buy; you may cancel at any time, even after receiving your free shipment. Simply complete your details below and return the entire page to the address below. **You don't even need a stamp!**

YES! Please send me 4 free Special Edition books and a surprise gift. I understand that unless you hear from me, I will receive 6 superb new titles every month for just £2.90 each, postage and packing free. I am under no obligation to purchase any books and may cancel my subscription at any time. The free books and gift will be mine to keep in any case.

E3ZEF

Ms/Mrs/Miss/Mr ....Initials..
BLOCK CAPITALS PLEASE

Surname...

Address...

....

....Postcode ....

Send this whole page to:
UK: The Reader Service, FREEPOST CN81, Croydon, CR9 3WZ
EIRE: The Reader Service, PO Box 4546, Kilcock, County Kildare (stamp required)